Handy Andy **SAVES** THE **WORLD**

Jackie,
Great meeting
you!

E.J. cckuch

BOOKS BY

EJ ALTBACKER

Handy Andy
SAVES THE WORLD

EJ ALTBACKER

Contents

Printed in the United States of America

First Printing, 2015

Print ISBN: 978-0-9863113-0-7
eBook ISBN: 978-0-9863113-1-4

Cover Illustration Copyright © 2014 by Hillary Bauman

www.EJAltbacker.com

prologue

"Senior Scientist Jarem, personal memoir. Begin playback of video for posterity."

Inside a tight communications bay, Jarem watched a small monitor. On it, an oblong spaceship slid through the blackness of space, its hull scales rippling and changing color as it glided on the delicate solar currents, making the craft appear (to an Earthling, at least) like a deep sea anemone traveling in a sparkling ocean.

Jarem caught his reflection in the monitor. His soft green fur was matted and his once smart uniform was rumpled and soiled. He sighed, causing his antennae to droop. "For thousands of years, the citizens of the benevolent planet of Oort have traveled throughout the galaxy." His kindly alien voice was punctuated by low purrs. "We had once again discovered sentient life and, as is our way, journeyed to this world to bring peace."

On the monitor something zipped past the craft too fast to be seen. Then another, and another. Meteoroids. The ship hit its thrusters and slewed sideways, as a slower, but infinitely larger, rock crossed its path.

"Impossibly, and for the first time in recorded history, an Oort peace mission has ended in abject failure. This ignoble and lamentable result was due to the incompetence of a single one of that planet's more than seven billion inhabitants." On the monitor the colorful spaceship was engulfed in a meteoroid storm. It dodged and weaved but was struck. The wounded craft tumbled into the sparkling void and the unseen camera went to snow as it was obliterated.

Jarem shook his head. "The planet is called Earth. The inhabitant who ruined everything was a male of the species with the ridiculous name of *Andy.*"

Jarem ended this sentence with a hard purr, which sounded very much like a fart.

one

Andy Robinson was inside a metal duct with a small flashlight clenched between his teeth. The heat plastered his hair against his face. A threatening buzz vibrated the metal around him. He moved forward a small distance and reached an old compressor caked in grime. Carefully Andy got his hands in front of him and wiped the sweat from his eyes. The metal duct ticked and groaned from his weight and movement. In the little space available Andy grabbed the pouch hanging from his neck. It unrolled into an expert set of tools that had everything he needed.

A voice echoed to him through the duct. "Let me call for help."

Andy took the flashlight from his mouth and turned to reply—banging his head solidly on the side of the duct, causing a low *bonnng* sound. He shook his head at his stupidity before answering. "I told you I got this."

In quick succession, Andy used his hammer and chisel, ratchet, electric screwdriver, crimper, and finally a wrench to disassemble the casing in front of him. The pitch of the compressor grew uneven. The machine let out a series of metallic coughs.

That was bad.

The echoing voice behind him grew frantic. "For God's sake, get out of there. It's not safe!"

Andy didn't look back to answer. "That's what you pay me for." He jammed the flashlight into his mouth and with no hesitation plunged his hands into the sputtering machine guts. After a few careful adjustments the sounds subsided, all except the low hum vibrating the duct.

Andy whispered, "I have you now," as he brought forth a small wrench. This job was important. He must succeed. Andy tightened one particular nut and the vibration stopped. He listened warily for a moment before smiling in grimy relief.

"See? No problem. Just a matter of—"

HSSSSSSS! Andy was cut off by a high-pressured whistling.

The voice outside yelled, "Get out! Fire in the hole!"

Andy struggled to retreat, but was stuck fast. In the gloom of the metal duct he cast his light toward the compressor as the whistling grew into a shriek. His eyes widened right before the muted *FWUMP!*

Everything went black.

Andy gagged and choked as. . . the sound of distorted laughter filled the duct.

Just great. Everyone was watching. Not that Andy could see, but he certainly heard the dozen sweaty machinists who had abandoned their lathes and grinders and were now gathered by the air conditioning duct that he was trapped inside. Andy tried to free himself by strenuously scissoring his legs back and forth. It didn't work. "Guys? Little help?"

Hank, the foreman of A&S Machining, sighed. "Al, Bob. Pull him outta there."

Andy was yanked from the duct. His upper body was coated in the blackest of black soot.

"He looks like Wile E. Coyote after something explodes in his face," said someone, causing laughter. Andy couldn't be sure who. Then the compressor came to life, its gear teeth grating and snapping. Finally, it gave up the ghost and died. The workers' humor vanished and they all groaned.

Foreman Hank none too gently squirted a bottle of eye wash into Andy's eyes. "What did you do?"

"Umm, you know, Hank, that's supposed to be administered with less force—"

"*What* did you do?" Hank asked, but louder.

"The compressor wasn't running very well, so I—"

The eye wash worked and Andy could now see Hank jut his hand out like a traffic cop to stop him from talking. "Did I ask you to fool with the compressor? No, I did not. You see, my dirty air conditioner was leaking refrigerant, but working. This air conditioner with the broken air compressor you've created doesn't run, so now we get to work in a sauna. Are you happy?"

Andy couldn't bear losing another client. He put a hand on the foreman's shoulder. "I can fix this, Hank. You've been a valued customer for forever. Let me make it right."

Hank considered this until he noticed that Andy's hand had left a jet black imprint on his crisp white shirt. He pointed at the door, too angry to speak. Andy gathered his tools and packed up his trusty red toolbox. He left a trail of soot as he took a walk of shame past the glaring workers of A&S Machining. Though Andy was (unfortunately) used to these situations as of late, the filth that coated him didn't stop a hot prickle of embarrassment from raising the hairs on the back of his neck. He nodded to each glaring machinist in turn as he left.

"Mike, John, Al, Steve, Bob. . . "

Andy left the building to a picture-perfect day in Sienna, Colorado. This contrasted nicely with his mood, which was dark enough to match his soot-covered skin and clothes. The small town was surrounded by forested hills and had its own leisurely pace which Andy loved, even if it was a little dull.

He heaved his toolbox into his battered pickup, Justine. Andy's father, Andy Sr., had given the truck her name. Painted on Justine's dented door was "Handy Andy," with a logo of a cartoon handyman holding a toolbox low in one hand and the world over his head with the other. "World's Best Handyman" was arched over that. His father may have overestimated his abilities on the day he created the logo, but Andy wasn't about to change it now that his father was gone.

He was in the middle of cleaning himself with a rag—digging deep into his ears and up his nose—when a loud *HONNNK* caused him to jump in what had to be a comedic way for anyone lucky enough to be watching. Andy frowned at the shiny Mister Fixx-It van that drove by, but waved instinctively. It was a small town and most everyone knew each other. It wouldn't do to be rude just because he was having a bad day.

"Lookin' good, Andy!" shouted either Ricky or

Doug—probably Ricky—as they roared past. Mister Fixx-It was a franchise with a fleet of repair vans that had expanded into Sienna several years ago. They had been munching away at his business ever since.

Andy got into his truck and drove. Justine sputtered her way down the street. Andy had been experimenting on the truck for years, hoping to light upon something great. It ran on used cooking oil, but not well. He passed several fast food places interspersed with Mister Wu's Dry Cleaning, Ken's Gas, and Emma's Diner. As Andy stopped for a light by the town's small police station, Justine backfired, sounding alot like gunshots. Sheriff Ralston, a no-nonsense ex-Marine and Vietnam veteran, tensed into a crouch. The younger and jumpier Deputy Bob dove to the ground. Both shook their heads when they saw it was him.

"Sorry, Sheriff. You too, Bob."

The light changed and he continued on his way, the prickle of shame returning in force. Andy sighed. He'd tried so hard to be a good businessman like his father, but was feeling more and more like a joke that everyone in town shook their heads about. When would it end?

two

Andy parked his pickup on the left side of the driveway where he had laid out cardboard to catch the numerous leaks from his prototype cooking oil engine. His wife Lynn didn't like having cardboard on the driveway, thinking it made their place look low rent. She was probably right. That Lynn allowed it because she knew what Justine meant to Andy was one of the too-numerous-to-count reasons why he loved her with all his heart.

The engine knocked for a ridiculous amount of time after Andy got out and closed the door. Finally, as he was almost to the house, Justine let out a ping and sighed. In the following silence Andy heard vegetable oil drip onto the cardboard.

One day he'd get it right. One day. He went up the steps and into his house.

"Daddy!" Just like every other day, Andy's adorable eight-year-old son Danny tore over to meet him. He held out his hands as a barrier so Danny wouldn't take a flying leap into his filthy arms.

With Danny parading behind, he tiptoed to the washroom, trying in vain not to spread soot. "Hold on. Just a minute." It was for situations like these that Andy had turned a downstairs half bath into a washroom. The repurposed space had a slop sink and pegs for his work clothes. It was painted a cheery green, and kept his work mess out of the rest of the house. Most days, but not ones with an overenthusiastic son in search of a daddy hug while he was covered in soot.

Andy kept Danny away with his leg the best he could as stripped off his shirt. His son, unfortunately, treated this like a game, and tried mightily to get to him.

His daughter came partway down the stairs and wrinkled her nose at the scene. "Mom, Dad's all gross again! Emily was twelve years old, going on teenager. "And why were you near my school? We've *talked* about this."

"Emily, I go where they need me."

"Gina said she saw you on the street picking your nose with a gross rag."

"Yuck!" laughed Danny. "Did you really?"

"No, I did not," Andy said.

In the mirror on the door, Andy saw his wife look down the hallway from the kitchen, her hands full with preparing dinner. She had her hair raggedly tied in a pony-knot (her name for it) and flour on her face. She couldn't see Andy but yelled down the hall, "Don't spread any mess!"

This distraction gave Danny the opening he needed to hug a filthy pants leg. Everything his son touched next, including one side of his cherubic face, was quickly smudged black. "Oh, Danny," Andy said. He reached for his little boy, who quickly switched the game to keep-away, running in circles in the hallway.

Emily continued to focus on what she thought was important. "You're totally embarrassing me. Stay at least three miles from school. Please. And Mom, Danny just ruined his new shirt on Dad's disgusting pants."

Lynn turned and saw them both. "Oh, Andy, you're kidding. And Emily, stop being a tattletale."

Andy scooped up his giggling son. "I have it under control." He looked at his daughter, perched dramatically on the stairs, the better to showcase her disapproving look. "By the way, how's your science project going?"

Emily became self-conscious. "Umm, good. But the teacher said we can't have parental help."

Andy acted like he didn't care, but did. He loved being a part of his kids' projects. He carefully picked up a few of the larger bits of soot in the hall. "Who's even offering? Not me."

Emily watched for a moment before asking, "Have you ever heard of space camp?"

Andy looked up from his cleaning. "Space camp? What's this about?"

"Gina thinks they'll meet boys," said Danny.

Andy chuckled as Emily stared daggers at her little brother. "Stop listening to my calls, brat!"

Danny stuck his tongue out as Emily stomped upstairs. Andy tickled his son, sending him into a fit. "Let's go clean up. You get in the tub and I'll take the shower. We'll race, okay?" His son nodded and gave him a salute before tearing up the stairs.

With the help of industrial scrubbing soap, a surprisingly painful twenty minutes later a clean Andy walked into the kitchen in time to see Lynn chopping the last of the vegetables like an Iron Chef. She had played soccer in college and it showed in little ways in the everyday things she did. For instance, she could dust like an acrobat. Andy had been lucky enough to meet her one day when she was coming off the practice field at UC Boulder and they had clicked.

Lynn gave him a mock-serious look, pointing with the knife. "I warn you, I'm trying something new with the rice pilaf. There are seasonings involved." She slid a catalog off the counter and into the trash.

"Consider me warned." Andy picked the catalog out of the trash before Lynn could dump a load of peelings onto it. It was open to a page featuring gleaming dishwashers. "If you want one, we can get one," he said.

"Too loud." Lynn kissed Andy, and without a word handed off various dishes as she finished the salad. This was done smoothly and without thought, a kitchen ballet they had perfected over the years.

They were interrupted by a door slam from upstairs, along with muffled arguing between the kids. The assembly line of plates was disrupted. They heard Danny shout, "Stay on your side, Lame-O!"

Andy pitched his voice toward the ceiling. "Emily, Danny, come down for dinner."

Lynn rubbed him on the shoulder. "So, what happened?"

"Nothing. Did you hear something happened? Does *something* have to have happened?"

Lynn grabbed his lips, scrunching them for a moment before letting go. "I only ask because it looked like you were in a coal mining accident."

Upstairs, Emily yelled, "Booger-face, give it back!"

Andy sighed. "It was a very dirty air conditioner. And I looked like an idiot. Again. I just can't seem to get a break."

Lynn took his hand, twirling underneath it. "Why, sir, I didn't know I was invited to a pity party. May I have the first mopey dance?" She pulled the biggest frown she could, but her eyes smiled.

Pretty soon Andy did too. He drew Lynn close. "You know I hate it when you sweet on my sour. Fine, let's talk about anything else. Kids, dinner."

"I'll bet you forgot Sienna Spree is this weekend."

Andy groaned and pantomimed stomping his feet like a pouty child. "Didn't we just do that?"

"That was last year. Quit being a baby." Then she shouted upstairs. "Kids! Now!" Like magic, Danny and Emily appeared at the table. Lynn gave him a shrug. "I'm the bad cop," she said in explanation.

Even though (as usual) the kids ate their food like starving prisoners and disappeared from the table in record time, family dinner was the highlight of Andy's day. Along with that came the nagging wish that he could just once bring home some spectacular news to keep everyone seated. It had never happened, of course. He had some funny stories, like when he was dyed blue fixing a defective Slurpee machine. Danny had made him tell that story ten times and Lynn and Emily had laughed so hard they snorted, which was apparently a cute quirk passed down from mother to daughter in their family. And he had fixed the machine in the end.

Today? He couldn't have talked about anything that had happened without wincing.

"The seasonings were an unqualified success," Andy said, earning a smile from his wife. They finished washing the dishes and he watched a little Sportscenter. At least the Broncos were looking good.

Before showering once more, Andy checked on Emily and Danny. By mutual agreement their room had been divided down the center with masking tape. Andy thought it was dumb, but Lynn had won him over to the idea. Let the kids figure it out for themselves, she thought. It did seem to lessen the number of ticky-tacky arguments between the two. Emily's neat half was plastered with tween-girl stuff while Danny's messier side had toys (lotsa Legos!) everywhere.

"How's everyone? Up to no good?" he asked, after knocking.

Danny held out his handheld video game. "I dropped it. Can I get a new one?"

Andy looked at the toy and sighed. Its case had been cracked, but at least still worked.

"How about I fix this one and we get a new one for

Christmas?" Danny was a little disappointed, but nodded. He grabbed an action figure off the floor and played with that.

Emily fiddled with her science project, a volcano with a small village at the base. The ingredients for the eruption sat nearby on the desk.

Andy peeked over her shoulder. "Need any help?"

"Let him. Daddy'll make it go boom," said Danny.

He gave his son a wounded look. "Daddy will not make it go boom."

Emily slid the project closer to herself, blocking his view. "You can't help, remember? Rules. Besides, I should do it myself. I'll learn more that way." Andy pushed aside a colorful curtain around his daughter's bed so he could sit by her side. Lynn had hung it so Emily could be alone, away from Danny, reading by flashlight or talking on the phone. It didn't always work, but Lynn insisted that a twelve-year-old girl needed some privacy from her little brother.

Danny wanted to come over to join them, but couldn't. Volcano, bed, and desk were on the other side of the room, and the masking tape line on the floor was the law. Emily nodded to emphasize the point. "Remember what happens when you cross the line, booger-face."

Danny frowned, but went back to his action figures. "Like I'd ever want to be on your loser side."

"Don't call your brother a booger-face and don't call

your sister a loser," Andy said. He paused and glanced past Emily at her project. "So you decided to go with the volcano. . ."

"I know you wanted to do a mini-helicopter, but the teacher said that would be way too dangerous."

"Your teacher is a weenie," Andy said. "There will be five other volcanoes. Don't you want yours to be best?"

Andy saw Lynn in the doorway, smiling at this exchange. "Emily, if you want to sleep over at Gina's tomorrow, help me today," she said.

Emily slid the project to the farthest corner of the desk and followed Lynn out. She gave Andy a warning glance before she left the room. "Don't touch it."

"Of course not," he said. When Emily left he took a closer look at the project. If you were going to do a volcano it needed to be spectacular. Andy could see the reaction chamber wasn't nearly big enough to make that happen. He had a few things in his toolbox that could make the difference, though. He could probably fiddle with it after she went to bed. His little girl slept like a rock.

If a father could help his daughter turn a B- project into an A+ one, wasn't he obligated to do so? Why, Andy would probably be thought of as a terrible parent for *not* doing it. He turned to his son, still trapped on his side of the room. "You think I should help, don't you?"

Danny nodded eagerly. "Definitely."

three

The next day Andy successfully repaired a balky water heater and what turned out to be a horribly clogged, but not broken, disposal before noon. With that done, he elected to treat himself to a slice of apple pie a la mode at the tail end of lunch at Emma's diner. After paying and stopping to chat with Emma (also a client for years) he was off to see Emily's science fair. Andy was excited. With his minor adjustments—done in the middle of the night when everyone was asleep—her volcano should really stand out.

As he left the diner Andy noticed signs reminding

people that it was "Sienna Spree Time!" and to "Buy Tickets Now!" He frowned. The town of Sienna was chatty enough. It didn't need everyone gathered together to trade stories, some of which would undoubtedly feature his sooty failure at A&S Machining. Andy walked into the parking lot and immediately noticed the red Porsche was parked next to Justine, along with a couple of Mister Fixx-It vans.

Great.

The owner of the Porsche was Andy's brother-in-law Kyle. Kyle was handsome and successful, a big fish in the small pond that was Sienna. He was also a rude jackass who didn't mind saying how lucky Andy had been to marry his sister along with how *unlucky* she had been for that same reason.

Andy tried to slip into his truck without being seen. Unsuccessfully.

"Nice job at A&S, Andy," said Todd, one of the Mister Fixx-It repairmen. "I hear it's a hundred and fifteen in there." Ricky, Kyle, and Doug were also there. He had known them all for ages. The repairmen chuckled good-naturedly (for the most part) at Andy's palpable discomfort.

Kyle turned to Ricky and Doug. "Why didn't they call you guys?

"Hank and Andy's dad were best buds," said Doug.

Andy waved a finger, disagreeing. "That's only part of it. Mister Fixx-It doesn't work on industrial air conditioners."

Ricky imitated Andy's finger wave. "Not until next month. Boss just hired a specialist from Denver."

Doug punched Ricky in the arm. "Don't give bad news and enjoy it. Makes you kind of a jerkwad."

"It's fine." Andy tried grinning, but it came off as fake. This wasn't good news. "Well, you still don't do sprinkler systems and a bunch of other stuff. I'll be fine."

"Until a Mister Sprinkler System opens up," said the ever-unhelpful Kyle. He opened the Porsche's hood. "You want to see something that works?" Andy found himself drawn to the gleaming engine. Kyle held out a hand. "Whoa, not one step closer. I don't want my car to sound, or smell, like yours."

Andy ran a protective hand over his pickup's hood. "Hey, Justine runs on used veggie oil. When I get the bugs out—"

Kyle interrupted, "We'll be flying Jetsons cars."

Out the side of his mouth Todd said, "Sheriff's comin'."

Kyle and the rest quieted down as Sheriff Ralston opened the window of his cruiser. "Got a complaint about a red Porsche racing around the abandoned warehouses. Know anything 'bout that, Kyle?"

His brother-in-law feigned innocence, although Andy was pretty sure it had been him. "Me? No. I mean, I own a red Porsche, obviously, but it's a popular color. Probably kids."

The sheriff tipped down his mirrored glasses—yep, he still wore them—and gave them all a look. "Well, those *kids* can expect a boot up their ass if I catch them. Savvy?" Ralston drove off. When he was gone the guys cracked up.

Andy was glad for the interruption, as it gave him time to get behind the wheel of his truck. He started the pickup, which promptly stalled. Kyle and his friends laughed even louder.

"It still has a few bugs," Andy said, as he turned the engine over until it caught. He found himself thinking about high school and what a bullying idiot Kyle was back then. And here it was twenty years later and, while he wasn't exactly a bully, Kyle still had the same dynamic with Andy. At least he didn't wedgie people anymore.

Or if he did, at least Andy wasn't the one being wedgied.

It was a short ride across town to Emily's school. He parked Justine and went inside the gym. There was a science fair, all right. Parents, teachers, and kids walked between aisles of projects with easels, ecosystems, models, maps, pegboards, and other props.

Andy weaved through the crowd until he found Lynn

and Danny. "Where is she?" he asked. "Has she gone yet?"

His wife pointed to a row of tables Andy hadn't seen. Sure enough, there were many other volcanoes. A boy in line before Emily set his off. Baking soda lava dribbled out of it in front of the judges, the principal, and a couple of teachers. Andy and the other gathered parents clapped politely. He leaned over to Lynn. "Ha, that's a loser. Wait until Emily's gets going."

Lynn saw Andy fist bump with Danny. "Please tell me you didn't do anything."

He was about to say something not-exactly the truth when Danny said, "Daddy helped." Lynn shook her head and he fell silent. It was Emily's turn, anyway. His wife would see soon enough that he was right.

Principal Brennan, a rotund and perpetually tense man, nodded at Emily. She added her eruption mixture—on top of what Andy had stacked inside. The volcano gurgled and spouted a nice gout of "lava" toward the papier-mâché town. It also poured out a thick pillar of smoke. Principal Brennan motioned for Emily to step back.

Lynn, now more worried than annoyed, gave Andy a stern look. He reassured her. "Smoke. Volcanoes do that. Makes it more realistic. And what do they tell us at the parent-teacher meetings? Get involved."

Lynn was about to say something when Emily's volcano let out a thunderous *BOOOOM!* Lava shot from the volcano cone to splatter on the ceiling twenty feet above.

Principal Brennan panicked. "Run, people! Run for your lives!"

The sprinkler system activated, dumping a torrent of water on everyone as they scampered for the doors. Alarms rang as soaked parents and children left in a semi-chaotic hurry.

Outside, Principal Brennan regained his composure and tried to make the best of the situation. "No reason to leave. We can give out the awards in the parking lot." Brennan shot a glare at Andy, standing with his dripping family. "To students who *earned* them without help."

Other parents threw out comments as they passed. "Nice job, Einstein," "Idiot," and "Way to evacuate the school, Andy," were the nicest of the bunch.

"Hey, that sprinkler sensor was set way too low," he said.

Lynn put a hand on his shoulder. "Let's just stand here. Quietly."

Danny rubbed his eyes, bouncing from one foot to the other, happy as a clam. "That was the most awesome science fair ever. Dad, you can help me on all of my projects."

Emily's eyes widened in anger when she heard this. "Dad! I told you. What did I tell you?" She saw her class-

23

mates talking, pointing, and chuckling at them. "You're such a spaz. Did you have to make me one, too?" Emily stormed off.

Andy wanted to go after his daughter to explain, but Lynn hung on to his arm. "Maybe let her be for now."

four

That night's family dinner was a lot less to Andy's liking as Lynn's brother had invited himself over. Kyle laughed—more like brayed—as Danny recounted the events of the day in detail, and asked numerous excruciating questions to stretch the tale out.

Kyle enjoyed it immensely. Andy and Emily, not so much.

Finally Danny ended the second retelling with, ". . . and a fire truck even came!"

Kyle adopted a goggle-eyed look and acted flabbergasted. "Wow, Danny, you couldn't have told that story any better." He turned to Andy. "And you—just when I think you can't possibly top yourself with another spectacular foul-up, you go and make a liar out of me. Kudos, and. . . wow."

Andy saw Lynn blow a strand of hair from her face. He had learned long ago this was an *I'm getting annoyed* sign. "Kids, go watch something on the DVD player," she said. Not needing to be told twice, Emily and Danny rushed from the table.

"If your dad installed it, watch you don't electrocute yourselves," Kyle added as they left.

Lynn slapped the table, causing coffee cups to bounce and spoons to clink. Her eyes blazed, wiping the grin from Kyle's face. "Enough."

"It's okay, Lynn," Andy said. "In a couple of days, I'll think this was funny, too. No biggie." She checked to make sure he was telling the truth.

Kyle fidgeted. "Look, Andy, I know you pride yourself on doing it all as a repairman, but that day is gone, along with eight-track tapes, rotary phones, and butter churns. Soon there won't be people like you anywhere on the planet except the Congo, and there you gotta know how to fix a blowgun. The guys at Mister Fixx-It like you. You could work there. At a company with a future. I could talk with them if that makes it easier. It's no trouble, and it's the least I can do for all the crap I give you."

Andy was puzzled by Kyle's sudden helpfulness. Then he noticed that Lynn wasn't looking at him during Kyle's speech. He could see shame in her expression. The two had talked this out before tonight. In fact, it was probably why Kyle over in the first place.

"Sweetie?" he asked.

Lynn looked at him. She had such beautiful eyes, and they told him how sorry she was about the whole thing. "It's just, you've been killing yourself lately," she said.

Andy still felt a flash of hot betrayal. His wife had gone to *Kyle* for help. But had he given her any other choice? Emily's project had sealed the deal. She was really worried about their future. The realization stunned him. Andy didn't want to explode at Kyle, and definitely not at Lynn, but he absolutely had to leave. He pushed his seat from the table and stood, stiff as a board. His words came out in a weird, clipped cadence Andy could do nothing to stop. "Kyle, thank you for the nice offer. I'm going for a drive. To think about the offer. Delicious meal, Lynn. Good talk. Back later."

It took twenty minutes to be outside of Sienna on a peaceful unlit road, far away from the dinner table and Kyle's nice offer. Justine purred (for a change) and Andy patted her dash. He pulled over to the side of the road and turned off the truck. It only knocked for a little while.

Andy got out, drinking in the peaceful night, and then yelled as loud as he could at the heavens. "Why? Why? Why? Who clears their kid's school with a science project? Only you! And Kyle gets to be an ass to me in front of my family? And then look like a big hero for having me close my father's business? I got an offer for you, Kyle—an offer of a punch in the face! A two for one, good anytime! Why is this happening? Doesn't anyone else deserve some bad luck? Doesn't anyone else—"

He was struck dumb when a colorful spaceship wobbled through the night sky above him. The craft was out of control, swaying as it passed barely a hundred feet overhead. It was quiet, but made an intermittent moaning noise as it flew. The ship disappeared into the forest with a muted crash. Andy's mouth remained open in mid-yell. He looked back to where the ship came from, then forward to where it had disappeared. He closed his mouth and moved toward his truck.

Andy pulled his small flashlight from his pocket and pointed it into the darkness. "Is this someone's idea of a joke? Ha-ha-ha people, pile it on." A curtain of dust gently seeped through the trees in the direction the spaceship had gone. "Really funny."

Andy took a tentative step forward. "Kyle? If this is a joke, I swear you will be taking my two-for-one punch offer," he said, but quietly. He moved forward, into the woods.

Shafts of moonlight lanced through the trees, eerily brightening the way. Andy snapped a dry twig and jumped like a scared cat, arms and legs flailing. Cursing under his breath, he got control of himself and continued deeper into the woods. There was a soft glow coming from behind the next rise. Andy got down on his hands and knees and crawled to the crest of the hill. He peered over the ridge and saw. . .

A spaceship.

An honest-to-goodness, otherworldly, spaceship.

The crash had caused it to dig a furrow a hundred feet wide for several hundred yards. Scales on the ship's hull rippled up and down in patches, as if the entire craft were a living thing, wounded and panting on the ground.

"No way," Andy whispered.

He let out a barking laugh, immediately covering his mouth to silence himself. He could not believe—accept— what was in front of him was actually real. He needed to be sure. Cautiously, Andy moved through the torn earth toward the ship. The ground was hot, steaming in a few places. A couple of shrubs were on fire.

Finally he was within arm's distance from it. Andy extended a trembling hand to touch the hull. When he did, the scales closest to his fingers moved and changed color, clicking softly as this domino effect continued down the ship's hull. Andy pulled his arm away, grinning.

It was incredible, unbelievable, and amazing. His terrible day had turned into the greatest day *ever*—maybe one of the greatest days *anyone* had ever had. After all, who else had found a space ship recently?

Then Andy heard the pitter-patter of something scurrying close by.

He whirled. "Who—who's there?"

Nothing.

Andy let out a suddenly tension-filled breath and turned back to the spaceship.

But it wasn't just the ship there now. Ten feet from the saucer's edge, a small alien stared at him. It was about a foot and a half tall and the cutest alien Andy could ever have imagined. It had short lime green fur with big eyes, two expressive antennae, and wore a jumpsuit uniform. He or she (possibly it?) was adorable. Still, adorable or not, Andy did what most anyone would do when alone in a dark forest in the dead of night, seeing an alien. He screamed.

"OH MY GOD!"

The force of this terrified yell caused the alien to squeak and zip away so fast it almost blurred. Andy clamped both hands over his mouth, trying to contain himself. He was frightened out of his wits! Hopping up and down, he turned around in a complete circle, searching for the alien which was now nowhere to be seen.

There!

Behind a stump of a sheared-away tree, the alien slowly rose. Andy first saw the antennae, then the big eyes, then the furry face. He remained motionless (more likely petrified), as the alien cautiously stepped out from behind its hiding place. After a moment of its fiddling with a colorful metallic pad in its hand, the metal disks on the collar of the alien's uniform flashed.

"Greeeeeeetingzzz," said the alien. It purred at the end of the word.

Shocked, all Andy could do was give a little wave and answer, ". . . hey." The alien lifted the pad and a dazzling rainbow burst of color stunned Andy, who stumbled around, flailing. It wasn't a ray, but more of a camera flash on steroids. "I come in peace. Please, do *not* probe me!"

When he regained his vision, the little alien was gone. Andy was scared. There had been enough adventure for the night and it was time to go. When he turned to leave, he bumped into an entirely different alien. This one was much taller than Andy: a severe-looking, bug-eyed, toothy beast that stood by way of a forest of tentacles underneath its body. If you had to describe this alien, the term "squid-like" would definitely be used.

A terrified moan escaped Andy's lips. While staring at the squid alien, he heard another sound, a mechanical twittering. It seemed to be coming from very close to his left ear. Andy glanced that way and saw that the little green alien had reappeared, and now stood on his shoulder. It was scanning him with the (obviously) multi-purpose pad device, which was making the twittering noises as it did whatever it was presently doing.

The smaller alien asked, "Is you sing-ging? Awww-ful."

The larger alien laid a slimy tentacle on Andy's shoulder. "Hullo," it gargled.

Well, there was no sticking around for this. Andy's paralysis broke in a major way. He ran like the wind, barreling through the forest. Branches whipped his face as he yelled unintelligible gibberish. He tripped and took a long rolling tumble down the hill, which spat him out of the trees near where he had parked. It was a wonder he didn't kill himself.

Andy ran to the pickup and skidded to a halt by the door. He dropped his keys, and solidly smacked his head on Justine's door in a rush to grab them. This staggered Andy, but he finally got inside the truck. He saw the squid alien come out of the woods in an unnerving, spidery way. It waved its thinner tentacles in the air while using the thicker ones to continue toward Andy.

The engine ground, but wouldn't start. "Not now, Justine, for the love of God, not now!"

The squid alien was less than a hundred yards away and moving at a good clip. Andy pulled the inside door handle off trying to open the door and get out. He rolled down the window, dove outside—landing squarely on his back—and sprinted down the road faster than anyone, including Andy himself, would have thought possible.

five

Andy got all the way to the park in the center of town before he stopped running. He saw that some booths for the Sienna Spree were already built and circled with saw-horses, ready to be set in place for the event. There were two painful stitches in his sides. Sweat had soaked his shirt and jacket, forming large stains under his arms, down his back, and on his chest. The shirt was more stain than shirt at this point.

Sheriff Ralston was speaking with someone and Andy limped over that way. "Sheriff! Sheriff!" he gasped. Ralston turned, revealing that Kyle and the Mister Fixx-It guys were the someones. Andy did an about-face and limped off in the other direction for a few steps. Could his luck be any worse?

"Of course they're here. Why wouldn't they be?" he muttered under his breath.

But he had to tell someone about what he had seen. Right?

Andy pivoted back toward the Sheriff. Kyle noted his disheveled appearance with a grin. "Wow, have I told you Lynn could have done much, much better than you?" Todd, Ricky, and Doug laughed. Apparently, this joke never failed with the fellas.

"Something the matter, Andy?" asked the sheriff.

"Can we talk? Privately?" This caused a few raised eyebrows from Kyle and the rest, but they kept their mouths shut. The sheriff guided Andy a few steps away and motioned for him to say what was on his mind. "I, umm—there was—how to put this—I saw. . . something. . . in the woods."

"What did you see in the woods?" The Sheriff asked loud enough so that everyone heard. He wasn't trying to embarrass Andy; he was a naturally loud talker.

Andy lowered his voice further so Ralston had to lean in to hear. "I saw, umm, what I mean to say is, there was a crash—"

The Sheriff grabbed the walkie-talkie Velcroed to his

shoulder. "Crash? Where? Was anyone hurt?" He spoke into his walkie-talkie. "Sue, stand by, we might need the ambulance."

Andy talked into the walkie. "No, no. No ambulance needed, Sue."

Ralston gave him a hard look and stuck the walkie back on his shoulder. "Andy, if this is an emergency I need to know. So tell me what's going on, ricky-tick."

Everyone gathered around. There was silence as the group waited for Andy to say something. Kyle had even shut up. Andy took a deep breath and said, "I saw aliens in the woods." The sheriff sighed, but Andy continued. "Look, I know it sounds crazy, but please listen. There were at least two."

"I believe you," Ralston said.

Andy had been prepared to do a whole lot more convincing. "You do?"

The sheriff nodded. "It's a problem everywhere."

Andy was confused. Shouldn't he have seen something about that on the news? "Really?" asked Andy. "It is?"

"But never call 'em aliens or you'll get looks," Ralston said. "They're 'undocumented immigrants' or 'guest workers.'"

Todd nodded, agreeing. "Yeah, 'aliens' sounds super racist."

"I don't think I've been clear," said Andy.

The Sheriff spoke into his walkie. "Sue, get Bob to meet us—where?" Everyone turned to Andy.

Much to Andy's chagrin, as Sienna was a sleepy town and there was nothing better to do, the whole gang came along. Deputy Bob met them there and they—Ralston, Kyle, Ricky, Doug, and Todd—gathered around Andy's pickup. It was less scary with a big group, but everyone was quiet.

"So, which way?" asked Ralston.

"Up there." Andy gestured up the hill.

Sheriff Ralston and his young deputy led the way with Andy. Kyle and friends followed.

"I think I hear mariachi music," Kyle whispered.

Andy's gut clenched. "Shh. It's just over the hill."

The sheriff looked over, skeptical. "You say these people crashed their vehicle a quarter mile into the woods, and over this hill?"

Andy nodded, knowing how it sounded. "It's better you see for yourself." About twenty feet from the crest, Andy got down on his hands and knees to cover the last bit. Ralston was dubious but did the same, motioning for everyone else to follow suit. There were chuckles from the others but they also crawled. Andy looked over the ridge along with everyone else, and saw. . .

Nothing but woods.

Everyone got up. The Sheriff wiped dirt from his knees. He took off his hat and rubbed his buzz cut, annoyed. "Damn goat rope. I did enough crawlin' around in 'Nam. Are you drunk?"

Andy walked around, searching, but saw nothing. "They were right here. Aliens—I mean, immigrants." The group watched in disbelief. Andy sighed. "Yeah. I was drinking."

The Sheriff grumbled and headed down the hill with everyone else. Andy took one last look and followed.

Lynn came outside as the tow truck driver disconnected Andy's pickup. Not wanting to miss anything, Kyle parked his Porsche on the street and hurried to join them.

"What's going on?" asked Lynn.

Andy didn't know where to begin. "I, umm, you see. . ."

Kyle shouldered his way between them. "Let me, I insist. Andy told the sheriff he saw 'illegal aliens,' his words, crash in the woods. We tramp into the forest but when we get there, Andy tells us he didn't see anything *and* that he's drunk."

"Is that true?" Lynn asked.

Andy couldn't meet his wife's eyes. ". . . partly."

"You're lucky Ralston's old and hates paperwork." Kyle told Andy.

"Kyle, it's late. Good night." She took Andy by the arm and they walked to the front door. "Let's get inside," she said.

Andy looked back to see his brother-in-law making an L for Loser on his forehead.

Lynn hovered between the fridge and cupboard as Andy gripped the backrest of a chair at the kitchen table. "Hungry? We have leftovers," she said.

Instead, Andy walked to their liquor cabinet and grabbed a bottle and glass. His wife watched as he sat and poured himself a drink. "I talked to them. There was this huge ship that turned colors," Andy said.

Lynn sat, reaching across the table to squeeze his hand. "So, they were towing a boat?"

"No one was towing a boat, Lynn," Andy said, raising his voice.

"Shh. The kids."

Andy calmed himself. "You know, I've given up on being the guy who invents something that changes the world, or even improves it a little, but this. . . I just don't know."

Lynn smiled. "It's okay to blow off steam. You had,

well, not the best day. You're putting yourself under too much pressure because of Mister—"

Andy held out his hand. "Please don't say the name."

Lynn nodded. "Fine. And my brother can be, well, a jerk sometimes."

Andy drained his glass. He got up to pace. "Sometimes. But he's right about one thing. You could have done better."

"Oh, please."

"If I'd finished college, I might be doing something that matters," he said. "Something you could be proud of. Me, I fix boilers. It was supposed to be one summer, but here we are."

"Hey, we started going steady that summer."

"I mean aside from that, of course," he said.

Lynn jumped into the gap. "You're missing the big picture. You're a great father, my loving husband, and we have two great kids."

Andy waved his hands around. "Great, everything's great. How did I miss the big picture greatness? I can't buy Danny a new Game Boy, much less a dishwasher for you."

"It was a catalog that came in the mail."

Andy took a gulp of his drink. "Emily wants to go to space camp. She could be an astronaut. Will we ever know? No. Because I can't send her. That's my big picture."

Lynn shook her head. "When you act like this it's, it's—"

"Sad? Pathetic? Loser-ish?"

"Annoying."

Andy took another drink, draining the glass. "I'll tell you what's annoying. Bringing the sheriff, deputy, your idiot brother, and his friends to see aliens and have them not be there. That's annoying."

Lynn sighed. "I really don't like that term."

Andy ground his teeth, trying to keep an even tone. "I'm not talking about people from south of the border looking for a better life. I'm talking about aliens from another planet. With a spaceship. From space." When Andy reached to refill his glass, Lynn grabbed his hand. She put the bottle in the cabinet, closing the door with finality.

"Really, Andy. If you can't talk about what's bothering you in an adult way, I'm going to bed."

six

Andy stared at the ceiling as Lynn slept peacefully beside him in the night stillness. He ran the past twenty-four hours through his mind. The chain of events caused him to (in order) grimace, shake his head, chuckle, silently strangle his pillow, adopt a look of baffled wonderment which turned into confusion. He sighed and quietly crushed the pillow on the top of his head. It had been quite a day.

He *couldn't* have seen what he thought he had seen. Could not.

Could he? No, it was impossible. It must have been induced by something. Could the seasonings that Lynn used on the rice pilaf have caused him to imagine it all? There had been nothing to see in the woods when he went with Ralston and the others. Nothing at all. Andy was dead sure he'd be reminded about that fact for the rest of his life by Kyle.

If it wasn't the rice pilaf, (probably wasn't) could hallucinations be caused by. . . stress? Or was he simply having crazy visions because he was *actually* going crazy? Neither explanation was anything that could be categorized as a good thing, that was for sure.

Or maybe Justine's engine was leaking some sort of vapor that caused a hallucination. Yes, that wasn't out of the realm of possibility. It was time to check the pickup's engine and tighten everything up. Maybe that would stop it from leaking onto the driveway.

And the hallucinations of spaceships and aliens.

Andy was about to cover his face with the pillow when thought he heard something go bump in the hallway. It was probably nothing. After all, if he was seeing alien spaceships, his hearing certainly couldn't be trusted, now could it? Andy got out of bed and went to investigate. He walked down the hallway, picking up and putting down his feet with care. Experience had taught him that the squeaky boards in the hall were loud enough to wake everyone if he stepped on them the wrong way. There was also the danger of skewering his foot on a forgotten action figure from one of Danny's expansive imaginary battles. Andy didn't see anything and was about to turn into the bathroom when a light pitter-patter noise sounded from behind him.

He whirled fast enough to cause his spine to sound off with a rapid pop-pop-pop.

Nothing there.

The kids' door was partly open, which was unusual. There was soft light spilling out from inside. Then Andy heard his son's low whisper. "Awesome. Can I try again?"

Getting closer, he saw that Danny was speaking with someone. It definitely wasn't how he spoke with his sister. Andy's gut clenched. Was there someone *else* in the kid's room?

He shook his head. That couldn't be.

Danny was talking to himself. Or sleep-talking? Or it was a computer program.

Something.

The pitter-patter sound moved from behind Andy and between his legs. When he craned his head in all directions—and there were no hiding places for anything larger than a mouse in the hallway—he saw nothing. This made things ten times worse. Andy opened the kids' door in search of logical answers. After all, there had to be a perfectly reasonable explanation.

But it wasn't reasonable. Not by a long shot.

A small, cute alien—different from the one Andy thought he saw earlier—uncoupled Danny's Game Boy from its own alien device.

His son looked at the alien and said, "Thanks, Lorel. This is the best." Andy's mouth hung open as he watched the little green alien scan his son while he played with his Game Boy.

Danny noticed that he was there. "Daddy, look at my new friends. Emily's gonna be so jealous," he said, keeping his voice low.

Andy closed the door, tension crackling in the air. He looked over at Emily's curtained bed and saw she was sound asleep. "Shh, Danny. Don't wake your sister," he said to his son.

"Like that's going to happen." Danny had face-painted his sister several times while she slept before the punishments got big enough that he stopped.

The tiny alien came forward and bowed to Andy. She did this perfunctory move so abnormally fast it froze him. "I Junior Scientist Lorel. I greet you. Please calm." Lorel's voice was that of a child's, interspersed with purrs.

"Right. Let's take it easy," Andy said.

"Good idea. *Eee-zee*," said another alien voice behind Andy, this one more masculine, but still childlike. Andy turned and saw an alien with a tiny ray gun on the shelf between Danny's action figures. It pointed the ray gun at himself and said, "Kezzek. Pilot Kezzek." This alien exuded cockiness and wore a uniform that was more of a flight suit. If the concept of *cool* was a thing with these aliens, Pilot Kezzek would be the coolest of the bunch.

Danny showed Andy his Game Boy, which had duct tape from where Andy had fixed the cracked case. A fantastic program ran on it featuring the cockpit of a spaceship with stars and planets whipping past the view screen above and below.

"Lorel says it's a program that Pilot Kezzek uses for flying practice. I crashed the first couple of times, but I'm pretty good now."

Andy nodded to Kezzek and then Lorel. "I choose easy. Easy," he told the alien in a hoarse whisper. Kezzek grinned and holstered his gun with a flourish. He jumped off the shelf, bounced on Danny's bed, did a flip, and landed on the floor without a sound.

Andy didn't know what else to do, so he knelt as his son played. "This one makes the ship go up and down, this one left and right, and here's the engines," Danny said.

"Boy, you're really good." Andy's eyes darted between Lorel and Kezzek. There are aliens in the kids' room, he thought dully. Would that affect the resale value of his home?

Pilot Kezzek took an interest in the masking tape line

down the center of the room. "What do line mean?" the pilot asked.

"It means the most awesome people in the world are on my side," Danny said.

Kezzek nodded. He said, "I awesome," and moved to Danny's side of the room.

Lorel showed Andy her computer pad. "Please to look and answer," she said.

On the screen was a picture of his pickup truck. She zoomed in on the Handy Andy logo on Justine's door. "You perform. . . menial labor?" she asked.

"Umm, I guess so."

"You fix space-ship," Lorel said.

Danny's eyes went wide. "Dad, they want *you* to fix their spaceship."

Andy loved Danny's look of amazement, but still— *aliens* were asking him to leave his home in the middle of the night. "There must be some mistake." he said.

Kezzek tapped the logo on Lorel's computer pad where it read, *Best Handyman in the World*. "No mistake. You best on planet."

"No, no, that's a logo. Lo-go," Andy said.

Lorel's eyes trembled and tears welled in the corners. "Please help? Menial labor?" Unseen by Andy or Danny she also gave a hand signal to Kezzek, who drew his ray gun. There was no need. Her eyes worked—on Danny.

"Daddy, they need your help. You always say we should help if we can. And you're the best handyman ever."

"Best handy-man," said Kezzek. "Righty-right."

What Andy wanted most of all were these aliens out of his house. If the price was taking a ride into the woods with them and being probed, so be it. "I guess I can go take a look."

Danny's excited whisper got louder. "Cool! Cool! Cool! Let's go!"

Andy put his hand over his son's mouth. "Use your indoor voice. And absolutely no way are you leaving your room in the middle of the night. The only way I'll do this is if you stay here. And you can't tell your Mom. Or your sister. This is top, top secret. Deal?" His son nodded and Andy removed his hand.

"Deal," he said.

Andy turned to Lorel and Kezzek. "Okay. . . take me to your leader."

seven

Andy couldn't risk waking his wife by starting—or more likely grinding—his pickup to life, so he elected to use his old bicycle. Kezzek perched on the front handlebar basket on top of his toolbox while Lorel clung to his shoulder. Thankfully, no cars passed them on the road.

Andy ditched the bike in a gully and walked up the crest of the hill with the two aliens. He saw no ship until Lorel used her pad and an illusionary curtain slid away to reveal the banged-up spaceship and ripped up terrain. So that's what had happened.

The first alien he had seen straightened from scanning a plant with his pad gizmo when he saw Andy and the others. "I greet yourself. I Senior Scientist Jarem. Why you run?" Now that he had met three of them he could see that this one was older, his green fur faded in areas. Certainly the title Senior Scientist would make him older than Lorel or Kezzek.

"I got scared," Andy said.

Jarem nodded. "Leader Kolgan speak at you."

There was a pop and whoosh as a door on the side of the ship opened and a ramp extended. It was like a classic science fiction movie which made Andy want to bolt, but he stayed put.

Kezzek said in a low voice, "First you meet Sub-Leader Nox." His purr at the end of this sentence turned into something like a raspberry.

Sub-Leader Nox wore a slightly different uniform than Lorel or Jarem with what Andy would have described as a modified dunce hat. He walked down the ramp, throwing colorful dust to either side. After that, Leader Kolgan appeared. His uniform was the most colorful and showy. He also wore a much larger hat of a different style—kind of a jester's cap. He strode down the ramp like he owned the planet.

Leader Kolgan hopped onto a stump and addressed Andy. "I great Leader Kolgan, nice planetary Oort. Speak your planet here." Andy didn't understand and he wasn't about to assume anything. His look of confusion was accurately read by Kolgan, who turned to Nox and gave him a haughty glare of disapproval.

"Not understand, stupid!" Sub-Leader Nox said to Jarem, and shoved him. He seemed to be Kolgan's attack dog. "Perform something."

Jarem's hands flew across his alien pad device. It turned several different colors, hummed, tinkled, and then gave off a triple purr. "Bonus words arrive," said Jarem. The Senior Scientist pressed a button on his pad and the collar disks on all of the aliens' uniforms flared for several moments.

Jarem cleared his throat with a purr. "By adding their world's 'internet' to our translators we can apply their most frequently used words and colloquialisms to precisely render our much more advanced speech in their crude language. Try it."

The leader of the aliens faced Andy. "I am Leader Kolgan of the benevolent planet Oort. I and my crew honor you by speaking your native language for as long as this world exists."

"Wow. We thank you. I'm Andy and this is Earth."

Leader Kolgan was perplexed. "Your world is called Dirt?"

"No, Earth, errrrr-thhhhh."

"Derrrrrrrr-t."

Andy nodded, not really knowing what to do. "Right, better."

"Well Dirtling Andy, my ship is damaged. I order you to do menial labor and repair it." Kolgan gestured to the shimmering spaceship.

Andy hesitated. "Are you sure you want *me* to fix it?"

Kolgan turned to Jarem. "It answered my question by asking me another form of the same question. Are you sure it's the dominant life form here?"

Senior Scientist Jarem thought about this. "Ah! Perhaps this particular Dirtling is stupid."

"Shall I *gazoortz* it, Leader Kolgan?" asked Sub-Leader Nox. Apparently there was no translation for *gazoortz*.

"Hey, hold on," Andy said as Nox drew his small ray gun from his holster—the only item that all the uniforms shared. "What I meant was I fix washing machines and boilers. Simple things. This is a spaceship. A real spaceship. You need someone, I dunno, a genius, to do it."

"But will you make the attempt?" asked Jarem.

"Of course I can try."

"Good, because I certainly won't," Leader Kolgan said. He laughed in a twittering purr.

Sub-Leader Nox joined in, laughing even harder. "Excellent humorous, Leader!" Apparently, Nox was also the alien version of a suck-up. In a very human way, Scientist Jarem sighed and rolled his eyes. Leader Kolgan went inside followed closely by Nox, then Lorel, and finally Kezzek.

Andy took a moment to stare in wonder at the amazing spaceship he was about to enter—or he would have if Scientist Jarem didn't then hop onto his shoulder and begin scanning him. Jarem waved his pad over Andy's head and it emitted a sprightly tune.

"Do you realize that your head is astoundingly large?" Jarem asked.

"I did not. . . realize that."

The Senior Scientist moved from shoulder to shoulder, at one point pushing off of Andy's nose to get at the back of his head. Jarem snipped off a lock of Andy's hair, took a reading inside his ear, then guided an instrument which popped out from the pad into his nostril which triggered violent sneezing.

"Umm, do you mind? We have a thing called personal space here," Andy said.

"I do not mind at all. We also have that concept. Delightful." Entering the spaceship, Jarem motioned for him to follow. Andy leaned down, slid his toolbox through the small opening, and crawled inside.

eight

Andy had heard of many things referred to as a wonderland: amusement parks, museums, wildlife preserves, and unspoiled medieval forests. But the inside of the Oort craft truly deserved that description. Soothing beeps and buzzes emanated from displays which were lit by neon bands built into the walls and the panels themselves. The sleek, high-tech bridge of the craft was at once futuristic and oddly retro. Above all, it had an undeniable simple elegance.

He was awestruck. Andy stood to take it all in—and hit his head ever-so-solidly. He was several inches taller than the ceiling. While the ship was fantastic, it wasn't fantastically spacious.

Sitting in his chair by the front view screen, Kezzek purr-laughed. "Easy where you stow your ginormous melon, Dirtling."

Andy rubbed his head as he hunched over to look around. Jarem and Lorel were at what he assumed were science stations at the back of this bridge. Leader Kolgan's chair sat on a raised dais in the center of the room with Sub-Leader Nox's chair lower and to the side.

Kolgan gave Andy an appraising look and nodded to Nox, who settled onto his own chair before speaking. "In the name of our great leader, I order you to perform menial labor now."

Kolgan purr-chuckled. "Nox, this is why you're only a Sub-Leader. No diplomatic skills, whatsoever. Watch and learn."

Kolgan got out of his chair, about to speak. He then noticed Nox still sitting on his chair, which put Nox up higher than him. Kolgan sprang up and knocked the Sub-Leader to the floor, startling Andy. Nox seemed none the worse for wear and bowed to Kolgan after getting up. The Oort leader continued, "I order you, Dirtling Andy, in a way you find pleasing, to repair my glorious ship." He purred, happy with himself.

Andy was determined to put his best foot forward for

the planet and the human race. "Okay, let me get to work, then. So—" All the Oorts turned their backs to him. "Hello? What are you doing?"

Sub-Leader Nox pitched his voice over his shoulder. "Being so stupid, your race might not understand this, but Oorts not only cannot do menial labor, we cannot bear watching it being done."

From his science station Jarem added, "To do so would shame us beyond belief. That's a scientific fact."

Leader Kolgan motioned with his hand behind his back. "Begin. Anytime at all."

Andy took in the colorful bridge of the spaceship with its alien gizmos and indicators. He had no clue what to do. Why would he? "Okay, where's the engine?"

Not turning, Kolgan tipped his hat. "I am right here."

Andy discarded several questions before settling on, "Do you plug yourself in somehow?"

"He says where we go and then we go," said Sub-Leader Nox. "I really think I should *gazoortz* him, Leader."

Kezzek pointed at his console without turning around. "Controls are at my station, Dirtling."

Andy put down his toolbox and jammed himself into Kezzek's tiny seat. The panels were seamless with no bolts or screws. "I need to take this panel off, then," Andy said.

"That's crazy talk," Sub-Leader Nox said. "You never take off a panel. Stupid Dirtling."

Andy bit back a reply. It was safe to say that Nox was his least favorite alien. He tried again. "Is there a manual I could look through?"

"Fix it, Dirtling! I order you," said Kolgan. Andy glanced at Jarem and Lorel, their backs still to him. Pilot Kezzek faced the wall and gripped a handhold.

"Well? We're waiting," Nox said.

Andy's hand hovered over one knob, then another, then a third. Finally he went back to the second one, which was green. Carefully, Andy twisted the knob ever so slightly. With a sudden hum the thrusters engaged. The spaceship majestically rose. Fifty feet up, near the tops of the surrounding trees, the engine cut off.

"Whoopsie," said Pilot Kezzek.

The spaceship plummeted to the ground, landing with a crash. There were flashing lights and angry twitters coming from every panel, most of which were now orange. The Oorts and Andy picked themselves up. Kolgan adjusted his large hat. "What in the name of Fronlak's turquoise exit hole did you do?"

Andy stood (momentarily forgetting about the low ceiling) and smacked his head again. "Mother of— how can I fix the engine if I can't see it?"

Kolgan hopped up and down on his chair like a petulant child. "I tell the pilot where to go, therefore I am the engine!"

Nox sneered, "It's a simple concept, you menial-laboring buffoon."

"Tiny, you're about to have a close encounter with my foot in your rear."

The Sub-Leader puffed out his tiny chest. "You want a sliver of me? I do not believe you could digest it."

Lorel adjusted her uniform. "Perhaps Dirtling Andy wants to examine the inner nodule?"

Senior Scientist Jarem nodded. "Yes, of course. Being from a backward culture the Dirtling seeks answers from the bowels of the ship, much like grubble worms on Oort diagnose ills by eating their own waste. Junior Scientist, make a note."

Lorel recorded this as Kolgan, Nox, and Kezzek reacted.

"Eww."

"Disgusting."

"I'm gonna hurl."

"I do *not* do that," Andy said. "And how can no one on your planet do any work? Who built the ship?"

Kolgan gave Andy an imperious look. "The machines did, of course. Machines take care of an Oort's every possible need from cradle to grave."

"Soooo, who built the machines then?"

The Oorts grew quiet. Jarem motioned to Lorel and the Junior Scientist took a ragged breath as if preparing to explain something particularly unpleasant. "There are two theories. The false one says prehistoric Oorts actually performed menial labor during a mythical period referred to as 'The Age of Embarrassment.' The correct theory maintains that the machines grew naturally from moss and various lichens."

Kolgan, Jarem, Nox, and Kezzek nodded at each other and Andy.

"That's the stuff," The Leader said.

Jarem agreed. "Scientifically vetted."

Sub-Leader Nox said, "Number two is true."

Pilot Kezzek added, "Dude."

It wouldn't help Andy to get into a deep discussion about this topic. "Moss, various lichens, right. So, where's this inner node?"

"Nodule. Nahhhd-jewel," Nox said.

Leader Kolgan purred, thinking. "Dirtling, for disgracing yourself by doing menial labor you may keep whatever you find in the ship's help box as a gift. Nox, give him the key."

Nox took a key off his neck and showed it to Andy as if he were the slow kid in class. "This is a key. Watch closely. Put this end in what's called the keyhole and rotate thusly. Once again, and thusly. Again. . . thusly." Nox repeated this until Andy grabbed the weirdly shaped key. Nox pressed a button on the wall and a dumbwaiter-sized panel slid open. There was a dusty pole there.

"Is this the only way down?" asked Andy.

The Oorts nodded. Andy sighed and climbed into the opening, gripping the pole. It was a thin shaft, but big enough for Andy to wedge himself into with his toolbox.

"And don't run away from Ron'nerlkjsdhfyerhfjlkejetc this time," Kolgan said, as the Oorts once again turned their backs on him.

"What's a—?" Andy realized they were talking about the *other* alien.

The scary squid one.

"Wait—that thing is down there? No way—no way—I'm going down there."

Without turning around, Nox pressed a button on his chair and the panel closed with a hiss, trapping Andy and leaving only a sliver open. "That is incorrect," the Sub-Leader said.

"Open this thing right now," Andy said, fear and anger rising in his gut. At least whoever had built the ship had included a light strip inside the access tube so he could see somewhat. Andy tried to pry the panel open. It wouldn't budge. Jarem backed toward him a few steps. "Dirtling Andy, there is no reason to fear. Ron'nerlkjsdhfyerhfjlke-jetc is a—"

Leader Kolgan purred threateningly and silenced the Senior Scientist. Kolgan said, "He's a harmless lesser animal, a pet we keep around. Pay him no attention. We shall let you out after you have repaired my ship."

Andy tried to get his legs underneath him, but his knees were jammed. "I'm stuck."

"I believe I have the answer," said Sub-Leader Nox. "*Un*-stick yourself,"

Andy gave Nox's back a look that could have turned him to stone. He pushed himself once, twice . . .

The third attempt sent him whistling down the pole. Andy landed on his back with a crash, his toolbox bursting open, his legs above him. At least the fall hadn't been too far. The floors of the ship were small. He felt around in the semi-dark and found a panel door similar to the one he entered and opened it.

"Well, that sucked," Andy said to himself after he tumbled to the floor. "Not like Star Trek at all." He was about to get to his knees when a tentacle slithered around his waist. Andy turned to see the squid monster as it pulled him toward its toothy maw and he promptly fainted.

nine

Andy dreamed that Lynn was hitting him with a wet sponge. He thought that this was an odd thing for her to do and was about to ask her about it but then the image faded away. Slowly, he came to his senses. He felt himself lifted to his feet and again saw the squid alien. It stood on its thicker tentacles while its thinner and shorter ones (arms?) hung on the outside, not quite reaching the floor.

If Andy could have shimmied back up the pole, he would have. He tried not to look at the beast. "It's a pet. Just a pet," Andy said to himself. "Easy, boy. Nice squid."

Andy picked up a screwdriver and threw it to the far

side of the room. "Fetch. Go play with the tool, boy. Play somewhere else. Far away." The squid alien turned to the screwdriver, then back to Andy. Its huge eyes, bulging from its head, blinked once—separately. First one and then the other.

"Hello. How do you do?" it asked. "My name is Ron'nerlkjsdhfyerhfjlkejetc. What is yours, human?" The words were clear, but there was a liquid gurgling noise underneath the speech coming from the alien's toothy maw. It extended an oozing tentacle, one of the thinner ones.

Andy threw another tool. "Get the Allen key, boy. Down the hall."

Ron'nerlkjsdhfyerhfjlkejetc bobbed his body once. "Am I not performing this correctly? Humans grip 'hands' when greeting, yes? My race opens our pouch to show if we are in mating season." With another of its thinner tentacles, Ron revealed a hidden pouch underneath its bulbous head. This looked and smelled like rotting fruit. And it was moving.

"Oh, that's. . . too much. Please close your pouch. Close it. Please."

Ron'nerlkjsdhfyerhfjlkejetc did so, but the other tentacle—held out for greeting him—remained where it was. . . waiting. A glob of something jelly-like dripped from it. With no small amount of anxiety, Andy gripped the tentacle with his own hand. "Shaking. . . hands. Wow, slimy and warm. That's different. Not a problem. I'm Andy. Nice to meet you. . . Rongalorflunchkin."

Ron'nerlkjsdhfyerhfjlkejetc's tentacles went rigid. "That is incorrect. Perhaps you could use a shortened version of my name and designate me 'Ron,' so to cease insulting my matrons."

Andy let go of the slimy appendage. "Right. Sorry, Ron. Your translator doesn't work as well as the others. Other aliens. You know what I mean."

"I'm not employing one. Each race in the galaxy has a gift. Ours is a skill for learning languages. I speak one hundred and sixty-eight. What is your race's skill?"

"No time for talk, Ron," Andy said, wanting to cut down on his squid time as much as possible. "Where's the inner nodule?"

Ron pointed a tentacle at a lever on the wall. Andy pulled it and lines formed from the floor to ceiling, dividing the wall into sections. These sections stacked to each side, revealing the engine. Twisty tubes filled with colored liquids formed a knot of sorts. No light or movement appeared to come from the device.

Andy looked over the engine. "Doesn't seem to have any power. Oh yeah, they told me there was a help cabinet. Where's the. . . ?" Andy scanned the engine room and saw a box with a single keyhole on the wall across from the engine. Ron stood next to it. ". . . help cabinet. Umm, Ron? Would you mind moving so I could get in there?"

The unappealing alien glided away in silence. Andy used the key the Oorts had given him to open the lock. Inside there was a six-inch baton with a single button on its side. Andy gingerly tugged the device from its clip. "Better be one heck of a tool, right? So, what do you do on the ship, Ron?"

"Answer one question to me, firstly. Why are you, a human, helping the Oorts?"

Andy shrugged. "Because they asked."

Ron bobbed its body. "Do you. . . hate your planet?"

"Umm, no?"

Ron weighed this and bobbed once again. It (He? Andy was beginning to think of the squid as a he) seemed confused. "Strange," Ron said. "In answering to your question: I am what you would call a butler. I was not always this. But that is not your business."

Andy nodded in the uncomfortable silence after this statement. "Okay, then. Let's get cracking." He walked toward the engine, holding the Oort tool. "So, just press the button? How can it do anything when I don't even know what's wrong with the engine?"

He clicked the button and the baton flared to life. Like a hydra, multiple appendages grew from the tip, lengthening and broadening far larger than the tube itself. "Holy moley! It's alive!"

The strands from the tool morphed into differently shaped heads that took apart and fixed the engine as Andy held on. All of these strands then flowed back into the tool, which once again became a small baton. The engine restarted. Or maybe rebooted. Andy didn't know. As the liquids moved, their colors became brighter. The glowing liquids flowed faster and faster until each tube emitted a musical hum, the tones of which melded quite perfectly. The colorful engine worked with a harmonious elegance that was amazing and otherworldly.

Andy was flabbergasted. The engine was a work of art. He stared at the workings of the spaceship's drive. "It's so simple. That's like a pool filter, that part is a condenser, wow. This thing is incredible." The wall panels slid back in front of the engine and became solid once more. Andy looked with wonder at the baton tool before putting it into his toolbox. When he did this, he felt more than a faint hint of disapproval from Ron.

This was borne out when the alien—in his clearest words yet—said, "You disgust me."

"They told me I could have it." Andy said, his own temper rising. He deserved points for getting through a remarkably strange night and not (totally) freaking out. The last thing he needed was attitude from a space squid.

In the end, Andy decided not to do anything. He didn't give a flying whit what this alien thought of him. "Have a nice life, Ron."

With that, Andy collected his tools and went back to the pole to return to the bridge of the ship. He thought he would have to climb back up, but the Oorts were waiting and wanted to know what had happened. They were very happy when Andy told them the news.

Getting up was made much easier by a seat that popped out from the pole—once Sub-Leader Nox pressed a button on his own chair, apparently. Andy could have used that same seat to be lowered into the engine room. Nox claimed he had forgotten about that feature because he himself had never been to the engine room. Leader Kolgan accepted this, but Andy saw Kezzek snicker and Lorel and Senior Scientist Jarem didn't look him in the eye.

Once outside Andy was treated to the fantastic sight of the Oort spaceship lifting off with a whisper, hovering, and landing again on its stubby legs perfectly before powering down.

Andy had made that possible. He had fixed an alien spaceship.

Eat that, Mister Fixx-It!

Andy felt so good he thought he could float himself home on pride alone.

"I have to go, Jarem, but thank you for giving me the

wonderful opportunity to fix your spaceship," Andy said, bowing to Jarem. "It will forever be the highlight of my working life."

The Senior Scientist gestured to the underside of the ship with his computer pad. Some of the outer scales were still damaged and one of the landing gear legs remained bent. "There are still various repairs to make. Can you not complete them?"

Andy got excited. "You mean it? You want me to do it?"

Jarem was baffled and made a note on his pad. "Yes, that is why I said those words. Dirtling Andy, I believe destiny has brought you to aid our mission of peace. By helping us, you'll change the future of your world.

Andy was a bit overwhelmed. "It would be an honor."

"I hope we can count on you to not tell anyone," Jarem said. "Other Dirtlings might not feel the same way." He glanced at Lorel, who stopped scanning things with her pad and moved closer to them both.

"Your secret's safe with me," Andy said.

Jarem hopped onto a rock. "That's good to know." Suddenly, he pointed past Andy's shoulder. "My word. Is that a carnivorous parakeet?"

As Andy turned to look, Lorel jumped up and clipped something to his ear. It stung. "Oww! What was that?"

Lorel ignored him and took a picture of a plant with

her computer pad. Jarem faced Andy with wide, innocent eyes. "To what are you referring?"

Andy fingered his ear. He could feel a disk about the size of a quarter hanging from a one-inch chain off his earlobe. "This. The thing Lorel stapled to my ear is what I am referring to!"

Jarem took a look and shook his head. "I don't see anything, Dirtling Andy. You must be mistaken."

Andy took out a small mirror from his toolbox. The thing on his ear looked like a funky earring. "I'm definitely not mistaken, because I look like a *pirate*. And I didn't look like a pirate when I got here. Is this a tracker or something?"

Jarem purred admiringly, making a note on his pad. "You have the intellect to suspect this? Delightful."

"Seriously, take this off."

Jarem took a picture of Andy with his pad. The colorful flash stunned him. "Take what off now?"

"Would you please stop doing that?" asked Andy, as he rubbed his eyes.

Leader Kolgan came out of the ship and, with Nox standing by his side, addressed Andy. "Dirtling, we continue to honor you and all others of planet Dirt by speaking your language for as long as this world exists."

"That's nice Kolgan, really, but I'd like this thing off my ear."

The Oort leader shook his head. "It's too bad you can't understand our advanced Oortian ways. Sub-Leader? Proceed."

Andy looked at Nox just in time to see him squeeze the trigger of his alien gun.

FZZZZT! Andy was struck by a ray. It spun him around and he fell to the ground. Jarem climbed onto Andy's prostrate form. He took a triumphant pose as Nox holstered his gun and took a picture.

Andy's foot twitched. "Make sure the Dirtling is taken back to where he came from," said Kolgan.

Nox bowed before his leader. "Forgiveness, but why let the Dirtling leave? It could compromise the peace mission."

"If it disappears, a gaggle of Dirtlings will search for it," said Kolgan. "Besides, Jarem wants to study it and scientists complain if they do not have things to study.

Sub-Leader Nox bowed again. "You are so wise."

"I know."

ten

Andy woke up fuzzier than he ever had before, and that included his bachelor party. He heard Lynn and kids downstairs. Everything seemed normal. But how could that be? It couldn't have *all* been a dream, could it? Andy shuffled to the bathroom. A shower would make him feel better. He bent down and scrubbed his face in the sink. When he straightened in front of the mirror, the dangling alien earring dropped into view, startling him. It had been no dream.

Everything came crashing back.

That little green jerk Nox had shot him with a ray gun!

The shiny disk dangling from his ear got his full attention. "Oh no, no," Andy said as he moved his head around, trying to get a better look. There was no clasp to be seen. The tracker-earring was firmly attached to the entire lobe of his ear, and sunk into the skin like a bloodsucking tick.

From downstairs, Andy heard Lynn ask, "Are you coming?"

"One second. I'm—I'm washing my face. Thoroughly." Andy grabbed the hanging disk in his clenched fist and took a deep breath. He would have to yank it off. Andy spread his feet, bit down on a hand towel, and pulled. This not only didn't work, it caused him unbelievable pain. After a high-pitched shriek that a passerby would have mistaken for a wounded bird, Andy grabbed a bath towel off the rack and screamed into that. The disk wasn't coming off without a good chunk of ear. Andy looked at it in the mirror. There was a slight trickle of blood. Then the earring glowed and the blood *stopped*. His ear even stopped hurting.

"What's going on up there?" Lynn asked from downstairs.

"Nothing. Don't come up. Private time." Andy attempted hiding the disk behind his ear. No good. There wasn't enough slack on the chain. It swung back and forth, mocking him.

"Breakfast is getting cold!"

Andy stared into the mirror, thinking furiously.

Andy cruised into the kitchen wearing one of Danny's knit skullcap with a superhero on it. Lynn was busy washing the dishes and Emily read a teen magazine off her iPad. Danny was engrossed with his Game Boy and the alien flight program. Andy hoped that Lynn wouldn't take an interest in that anytime soon.

The skullcap hid the alien device from view for now. If Andy was going to make his escape with no questions asked, he had to be quick. He picked up a bowl of oatmeal. "I'm gonna take this to go," he said.

Lynn didn't turn from the sink. "Don't be silly. It's oatmeal."

Emily's mouth fell open in horror when she saw him. Andy waved at her to not say anything. But no amount of signaling could keep Danny quiet. "Wow! Daddy's wearing my hat." Lynn laughed when she saw Andy in the too-small skullcap.

Emily wasn't amused. "Daaaad. You look totally lame."

"I think it looks awesome," Andy told his family.

Jarem stood behind Lorel as she tuned the controls at the science station in the Oort ship. Every one of the monitors was black, but the conversation in Andy's kitchen came through clear as a bell.

"He's right. It's totally rad," Danny said, his voice sounding from the darkened screens.

Lorel was puzzled, and flipped switches and adjusted knobs. "The tracking device diagnostic says it is working, but I'm not getting any video."

Head Scientist Jarem purred, thinking. "Interesting, I believe Dirtling Andy is attempting to stop us from gathering visual data. Get rid of the obstruction without harming it."

Lynn tried to get a better look at the alien earring, but Andy kept the table between them. He shoveled oatmeal into his mouth as quickly as possible. "Mmm, delicious. I can't stop eating this, it's so good. And I'm done." He slid the empty bowl across the table at Lynn who stopped it neatly before it reached the edge.

Andy headed toward the kitchen door but his wife blocked him. "Not that I don't support your decision to wear what you want, but do you think today's the best day to go around town in Danny's skullcap?

As he explained, Andy involuntarily began touching his ear. "Yup, I do. I feel a head cold coming on and, and—oh, *oww!*" The skullcap burst into flame by his ear. Lynn and the kids shrieked in surprise as he ripped off the hat and threw it into the sink. He ran water over it and his ear. After turning off the water Andy stood with his head tilted so the hot disk didn't touch his skin, revealing the tracker to everyone. "It's okay! I'm okay."

Lynn, Danny, and Emily fell silent when they saw the earring. Then his daughter said, "Oh. My. God."

"I can explain," Andy told everyone.

Lynn blew a strand of hair out of her face and folded her arms beneath her chest. Those were signs of double trouble. "Please do."

"I decided. . . this morning. . . to get an earring." The family was more than a little surprised by this news.

"What are you talking about?" Lynn asked.

"You're not wearing that in public," said Emily, shaking her head vigorously.

At least Danny was on board. "Can I get one too?"

Andy held out his hands for silence. "Okay, quiet down. Let me explain."

Before any explanation his son blurted, "Did the aliens give you that?"

Emily looked at her brother in confusion. "Aliens? What are you talking about?"

Lynn was quietly furious and took over the conversation before the kids could get further down that road. "It wasn't aliens, Danny. Aliens don't give you earrings. Bad judgment does." She shook her head at him. "I cannot believe you're trying to get the kids to believe your ridiculous story."

Andy struggled to come up with something. "This has nothing to do with aliens. Nothing. I was going to surprise you with this. And the surprising thing I want to tell you about is. . . that. . . I've been secretly working on, umm, a stylish, yet functional. . . earring for pets. Dogs and cats mostly, maybe birds. They would let an owner track their dog or cat. Or bird. So, tah-dah." Andy waited for everyone's reaction.

Emily gave him and the earring an appraising once-over. "Aside from how it looks—which is awful and embarrassing for a human—that's not the worst idea you've ever had. It's even pretty good. Jewelry for pets is 'in' now."

"Right, right. So true," Andy agreed. "She gets it."

His wife wasn't convinced. "It caught on *fire*."

"Exactly," Andy said. "That's called working the bugs out. I thought to myself—no way I'm taking a chance on hurting someone's pet—just no way. So I'll put it on myself to test it first. That way, for sure, no kittens or puppies will be set on fire. Or parrots. Not one."

"So, you can take that off?" Lynn asked.

Andy chuckled. It came out a little more manic than he would have liked. "Well of course, silly-kins. What type of inventor would I be if I couldn't get my own invention off? But, but—I don't want to do that because it would ruin my test if I took it off right this minute."

Danny beamed. "I bet you're the only Dad in town with one of those."

"Oh, I'd bet that, too," said Lynn, still not entirely on board.

Emily pouted. "I'm all for protecting kittens and puppies—birds are kinda gross—but do you really have to go out in public like that? Can't you test it around the house for the next week?"

"How about I try to stay away from your school," Andy said. He had no work coming up there, not after setting off the sprinkler system.

This cheered Emily and she shrugged with acceptance. "Fine."

Andy looked at Lynn and she gave him a tentative nod.

Good enough. He could work with that.

eleven

Inside the spaceship, Senior Scientist Jarem and Junior Scientist Loren watched on a monitor as Lynn shook her head disapprovingly. Since the camera was on Andy's ear, the Oorts only saw his hand or arm when it entered the earring's field of view. With their advanced technology Lorel was also able to separate Danny, Emily, and Lynn into their own individual feeds.

"What a delightful species," said Jarem. "Their dynamic is quite unusual. Dirtling Andy seems to fear the female of the species."

"Indeed, Senior Scientist," Lorel said. "This will make an excellent study."

An irritated Leader Kolgan passed the science station

with the Sub-Leader on his heels. "Nox, do you understand the concept of personal space?" Kolgan asked. When their leader saw Lynn on the monitor he stopped in his tracks, causing Nox to bump into his back. "Who is that bewitching creature, Jarem?"

The Senior Scientist consulted his pad. "The Dirtling's mate. I believe she is called Lynn. The smaller ones are spawn." Jarem made room for Kolgan to stare at the monitor over Lorel's shoulder. This wasn't enough for the entranced leader of the Oorts. He pushed the Junior Scientist from her seat, sending her to the floor. Lorel got up and bowed. Kolgan climbed into the seat and leaned close to the screen, fogging it with his breath. "Hoochie-mama. . . "

Outside the house Andy looked over his tools, which were still jumbled from the events of last night (when he had fixed a broken down spaceship, oh yeah). Andy knew the alien gizmo did all the work, but someone had to press the button. The Oorts had made it clear that they weren't going to do it. How weird was that?

Andy sorted other tools back into their correct spaces by feel as he searched the toolbox for what he needed. Gripping his trusty ratchet, he used it to reattach Justine's inside door handle that had been ripped off in his haste to get away from Squiddily-Diddily, also known as Ron. Satisfied with his fix, Andy got in the pickup and turned over the ignition. The truck wouldn't start. With a sigh, Andy popped the hood to find the problem.

Inside the spaceship, Jarem and Lorel finished lapping at their liquid ration cartons. Lorel took Jarem's when he was finished and threw both empty cartons into a waste chute.

They saw Andy's hands going back and forth from the engine to the toolbox.

"Hmm, what's it doing now?" asked Jarem.

Lorel's eyes widened as she realized. "Senior Scientist, doesn't Dirtling Andy's daily life consist of doing menial labor?"

Jarem spun away from the monitor. "Shut it down now!" Lorel clicked off the screen and the Senior Scientist sighed, relieved. "Excellent work, Lorel. I can't shame myself, even in the name of science. But you, you're a junior scientist. You can shame yourself all you want. Do some fieldwork and follow the Dirtling around. Write up a report so I can study it later."

Lorel grumbled after Jarem left. She noticed Kezzek grinning at her from his station across the empty bridge. "Kezzek, would you like to take a walk with me?"

Kezzek straightened in his seat, enthusiastic for a

moment. He then rethought this and adopted a much less eager slouch. "I guess it's better than sitting around on my furry green rear."

Andy tried the pickup's engine again. It wound and ground. "Come on, Justine," he said. Andy got out and reached for a spark plug tester. He stopped when he saw the Oort tool.

Hmm. . .

Andy picked up the baton. After a moment's thought he pointed the Oort tool at Justine and pressed the button. The baton scanned the engine and twittered for a moment, almost like it was thinking. It then developed twenty appendages and simply mauled the truck. Andy struggled, holding on to the tool with both hands as it swung him from side to side. "Oh my God! Oh my God!"

The pickup was lifted from side to side and at one point turned upside down. Every piece of the engine was disassembled, drilled, cut by torches and saws, heated and pulled into odd shapes, which were then reassembled. All during the process there were bursts of rainbow colors and sizzling noises.

Finally, the heads retreated back into the baton.

Andy stood there and panted. He had cried a little and wiped his eyes, checking to see if anyone had seen what happened. Other than birds, there was no one on the street. Andy tiptoed closer and peeked at the engine.

It had been *changed*.

Justine's engine was now like no engine he'd ever seen—no engine anyone from planet Earth had ever seen. It was a totally alien configuration that glowed in places.

"Whoa. . . "

Andy eased himself into the driver's seat and gently (very gently) inserted the ignition key. After a deep breath, he turned the key.

VA-RRRRRRRRROOOOMMMMM!

The truck settled into a fearsome idle, thrumming with power. Andy chuckled, which then turned into an all-out laugh. His truck was running! Not only wasn't it sputtering and conking out like usual, it was working like a champ! It would be a shame not to try it out. Cautiously, Andy pressed the accelerator.

The effect was shocking.

The truck left a rooster tail of asphalt and rubber as its wheels spun like a dragster's. Andy was pressed into his seat as if he were in a jet fighter. He was scared out of his wits and exhilarated beyond belief. He jerked the wheel this way and that, passing cars like they were moving in syrup. "Whoa, watch it. Comin' through. 'Scuse me." After a minute he got the hang of it. The speed at which he was moving turned the view from his windshield into a video game on the empty road. He cackled with glee and whooped. "Yee-haaa!"

Andy knew exactly where he would go next.

He strode into A&S Machining, sweeping past the sweaty men working at their stations, ignoring their disdainful looks. Foreman Hank came out of his office, but Andy didn't slow down. "Look, I got a little hot last time and I'm sorry, but I have a new air conditioner coming, so there's nothing for you to do," Hank said.

Andy put his toolbox down by the air conditioner duct he'd gotten himself stuck in the day before. He grabbed the Oort tool from his pocket and opened the metal duct nearest the compressor. "Then you have nothing to lose," he said to Hank, crawling inside before the shop foreman could say no.

Hank watched as Andy disappeared inside the short duct. After a moment there were noises: grinding, drilling, metal squealing in protest. "That's right, say hello to my little friend," Andy said, his voice echoing from inside the duct.

"What are you doing?" Hank asked. "I don't think this is a good idea."

Other machinists gathered around, most thinking they would be called to pull Andy out once again. Everyone stepped back as the various noises became a cacophony which got louder and louder. Some of the men held their ears. Then, just when it sounded as if something might explode, the noises stopped.

Hank walked tentatively to the duct and leaned down to the opening. "Andy, you okay? Should I get the first aid kit? Manny, get the first aid kit." Andy popped out of the duct, not dirty at all. As if on cue, the air conditioner started up.

The reaction from the sweating men was immediate.

"It's working! Boy, is it ever working," Manny said.

Another worker nodded enthusiastically. "It's like a Nordic breeze."

"How did you make it smell like fresh baked pie?" asked Hank.

Andy gave the foreman a hearty slap on the shoulder. Hank checked and saw that his shirt was still clean, unlike the last time. "It's on the house," Andy said. "Enjoy, fellas." He grabbed his toolbox and marched toward the door, head held high.

The machinists applauded as Andy left. There were comments thrown around: "Way to go, Andy!" "You da man!" and the like. The last—and sweatiest—guy gave Andy a cracking high five as he left the building in triumph.

Junior Scientist Lorel and Pilot Kezzek watched Andy go to his truck, a noticeable spring in his step. Lorel recorded everything with her pad device. Behind her, Kezzek was loaded down with her gear.

Lorel spoke as she filmed the scene. "Junior Scientist Lorel, notes on test subject Dirtling Andy. Subject's mood seems elevated from the experience of successfully completing a menial labor task."

"You said 'take a walk with me,' not 'be my pack mule,'" Kezzek grumbled, loud enough to be recorded.

"Quiet," she said, without turning around. "Dirtling Andy constantly shames itself doing menial labor but does not seem to notice or care. This puzzling behavior proves that Dirtlings are one of the most idiotic species ever encountered by Oortkind."

Kezzek stretched his legs and arms. "Seriously, my back is killing me."

Lorel filmed as Andy packed his toolbox into the pickup. Once she had him centered on the pad she turned, "Kezzek, can't you see I'm working?"

"You're super cute when you're cheesed off."

Lorel purr-laughed despite herself as Andy drove away. "We'll follow using the tracker," she said.

"It's just gonna go embarrass itself again," the pilot said. "We'll catch up to it later." He sidled up to Lorel.

"How about we sample some Dirt flay-vah? I liberated this from a cart on the street." Kezzek showed Lorel two churros wrapped in a napkin. The sugary rods were nearly as tall as the Oorts.

Lorel was aghast. "You know we're forbidden to eat or drink anything on a backwater world like this. It could be poisonous." She scanned the supposed snacks, frowning all the while. "They ingest this on purpose? Incredible."

Kezzek moved the treats away from the pad. "Don't be a dweeb. It's called a 'churro.' With a name like that, you just know it's gonna be good."

He moved one of the churros closer and closer to his mouth, smiling all the while.

"You're bluffing," Lorel said, shaking her head. "No way you'd eat that."

Kezzek gave her a devil-may-care grin and fed the churro into his mouth like a branch into a wood chipper.

She laughed, despite herself. "Fronlack's turquoise exit hole! I cannot *believe* you just did that." The scientist in Lorel got the best of her. "So? What is it like?"

"Hmm, tasty, sweet. Me likey," Kezzek said. "Oh, wow. Hold on. Getting something." Kezzek suddenly bounced off the two cars they were hiding between like a pinball.

"What's happening?" asked Lorel, worried. She drew her gun, changing a setting. "Should I shoot you in the mouth with a broad spectrum anti-poison dart?"

Kezzek waved this off. "No. This is amazing. I suddenly have the energy of seventeen Gracknals! I'm a whirlwind! Hee-yahhh! I can do anything!" Just as quickly, the pilot ceased his furious movement, winded. "Wait, wait. Now I don't want to do anything but take a nap. After another churro."

Lorel grabbed the last sugary rod. "No. I claim this churro for myself. And science." She ate the churro and ricocheted between the cars just as Kezzek had done. "Oh, I think we need to do more study on the foodstuffs of this planet."

twelve

After Andy fixed Mister Wilson's unfixable 1967 Ford F600 dump truck, he began thinking of this particular day as The Day of Triumph. And that was only his fifth successfully completed job of the day. After Wilson's truck he repaired Denny Pullman's ancient windmill, Miss Johanson's kiln, The Diobelli's underground sprinkler system, the balky pool filter at the high school (Emily had said nothing about the high school), Susan and Bob Losman's solar panels, and the fancy Italian coffee maker at Emma's diner.

It was a day of dreams. Sure, Andy knew that using the alien device was cheating—a little—but the Oorts had given it to him and he was using it properly. If he could be blamed for things that went wrong because of bad luck, surely he could take a little credit here.

And word got around town. Clients were *happy* to see him when he pulled up. By late afternoon people were calling him on his cell phone to come over. He ended up doing a few of the jobs for practically free, but that was okay. Andy figured he owed the town for all the things he had screwed up lately.

Plus, his Dad would have been proud.

For the first few jobs Andy tried to hide his alien ear-wear. But by the end of the day he was having so much fun fixing things he didn't care. He even got a few compliments. Yes, there were definitely more quizzical looks about the earring, but there were a few compliments.

What a day.

Andy never noticed Lorel and Kezzek followed him, which was exactly as they wanted it. Lorel needed her subject to act naturally in its environment to gather data for Jarem. She was fixated on the work at first, but Kezzek kept distracting her by liberating all sorts of delicious Dirtling treats from each place they stopped.

It was one of the most fun days she had ever experienced as a scientist.

They chugged cups of coffee, wrestled for Cheetos, fed each other candy bars, and shot Slurpees into their mouths at a wonderland called 7-Eleven. That was where Junior Scientist Lorel discovered the concept of "brain freeze," although she didn't know it was called that and named it (translated from High Oortian) *shockin' noggin' floggin'.* At the end of their own wonderful and productive day, she and Pilot Kezzek followed the Dirtling back to their spaceship.

Andy used the Oort tool to repair the damaged scales on the spaceship. Was there anything it couldn't do? And after that, he fixed the bent landing gear of the craft.

Day of Triumph, indeed.

Leader Kolgan, Sub-Leader Nox, and Senior Scientist Jarem were there—with their backs turned—when Lorel and Pilot Kezzek showed up. They also avoided looking at him while he worked, instead spending their time crunching a bag of corn nuts, which seemed odd.

Though none of the Oorts watched him work, Ron stared at Andy with a palpable anger.

What was the squid's problem? No matter. It was The Day of Triumph and nothing would spoil it. The alien tool's appendages finished their work and flowed back into the baton. "Well, that's it," he said. "Your spaceship is space-shipshape again."

Kolgan, Nox, and Jarem joined him. Lorel took pictures with her pad as Kezzek opened the bay on the bottom of the ship, looking inside. Both Lorel and the pilot were sporting paunches and sneaking snacks as they worked. The others didn't notice and Andy wasn't going to say anything, but Oort bodies could apparently pack on the pounds at an alarming rate.

Leader Kolgan beamed. "Excellent. You've done a great thing here."

"All in a day's work," Andy said. "And you really helped by giving me this tool."

Jarem hopped on Andy's shoulder and patted his head. "Come now, we could never have done this. Songs will be sung."

"Really? Actual songs about me?" Andy asked. It was so good to be appreciated.

Ron stared daggers with his huge eyes. "Yes. Songs of doom and destruction."

Sub-Commander Nox leaped at Ron and banged into the side of the squid alien's head with his feet. The blow had surprising force and Ron needed to shift several tentacles to regain his balance. "Hey freak show, go stick your head in your disgusting pouch." Ron gave Nox what Andy could only describe as a rude tentacle-gesture and scuttled inside the ship, gurgling under his breath in his language.

"That's right," Nox said. "Keep shambling away on those disease-ridden tentacles."

Andy tapped the earring dangling from his ear. "About this thing. . . ."

Jarem purred. "Oh, that will cease to be an issue soon enough."

"So it falls off once you're out of range or something?" he asked.

Jarem nodded, adding another purr of agreement. "Yes, it will vaporize completely."

Kolgan preened as Lorel took a picture of him in front of the spaceship. "And that will be in a few short hours," the leader said. "After Kezzek prepares the engines, it will be time to leave."

An alarm on Andy's watch beeped. "I've got to go, too. I have one more job in town and Lynn will kill me if I'm not back in time for the Sienna Spree." The Oorts didn't understand this. "It's a gathering where there are costumes, music, pie, and—never mind."

Andy was about to rush off when Kolgan solemnly bowed, with the rest of the Oorts following suit. "Enjoy the rest of your life, Dirtling Andy."

Andy awkwardly returned the bow. "Thank you," he said. "Thank you so much. Safe trip." He waved at the Oorts one last time and left their camp.

Kezzek turned and bowed to Kolgan. "We are ready to

begin the guide hole for the peacemaker, Leader."

Kolgan tugged the lower edge his uniform. "Make it so."

Before he left, Kezzek's stomach rumbled. Farther away, so did Lorel's. This got a look from Kolgan, Nox, and Jarem.

The pilot let out a nervous chuckle. "Must be all the fresh air and exercise."

Kolgan nodded, satisfied, and the Oorts filed into their ship. After a moment, an ominous hum built in intensity. Then a tight beam of green energy burrowed into the ground from the spaceship's underside bay, vaporizing the dirt and rock in its path.

thirteen

Andy came out of Wu's Dry Cleaning with the old owners happily following. The ancient Asian couple was beyond pleased. "I can't believe you fixed that stupid steamer," said Mister Wu. "It hasn't worked for years. Both Wus 'wuv' you! You see what I did there?" Mister Wu hugged Andy as his wife presented Andy with a check and a kiss on the cheek.

"You're a genius, like Bill Gates." Mrs. Wu said.

Andy reddened at the comparison even more than the kiss. "Jeez, that's too much, Mrs. Wu."

"Okay, you're at least as smart as guy who invent leaf

94

blower," she said. "That's for sure."

Andy headed to his pickup across the street with a spring in his step. He saw Kyle standing by his Porsche with Todd, Ricky, and Doug, and didn't try to avoid them. Not today.

Kyle gave him a condescending grin. "How's it going? Town still have power?" Then he noticed Andy's earring. "What the hell is *that*?"

"That would be my new earring, Kyle." Andy said this with such confidence that Kyle and the others were momentarily speechless.

Finally, Ricky said, "Looks pretty good."

"Pretty good?" asked Kyle. "He's wearing an earring. He's—" Whatever his brother in law wanted to say was drowned out by a resounding *VR-OOOOOMMMMMM*. All four men were mesmerized as Andy gunned his engine again.

"Couldn't hear you over my engine, Kyle," Andy said. "You say something?"

Todd laid a hand on the pickup's hood. "It's like there's a herd of rampaging wildebeests in there."

"Big deal, he finally got it running," said Kyle. "It's not like it can hold a candle to a real car."

"You mean like your little car right there?" asked Andy.

Silence.

Ricky, Todd, and Doug looked from Andy to the gobsmacked Kyle. It took Kyle a moment to recover his cockiness, but he wasn't one to back down. Especially to Andy.

"Oh, it's so on."

Kyle and Andy sat in their respective vehicles on the connector road by the industrial warehouse area on the outside of town. There was a chalk line drawn in front of their wheels. Kyle revved his engine and looked at Andy, making a throat-cutting sign from his car.

Standing between the two cars, Todd waved a wad of cash. "Okay, one time for two hundred dollars. Ready, set. . . go!"

Kyle's Porsche jumped off the line. Andy didn't move. He spent a moment polishing a spot on the dashboard. Satisfied, he winked at Todd and hit the gas. Justine screamed forward, hurtling like a bullet. It passed the Porsche with such force that Andy heard Kyle let out a shriek. Justine stopped on a dime just over another chalked line a half mile down the road, where the slack-jawed Ricky and Doug stood.

Andy didn't bother turning around. He gave the guys a grin and put his car in reverse. The truck went backwards as if shot from a cannon, passing the Porsche before it crossed the finish line. Andy threw his brother-in-law a jaunty salute as he went by, perfectly in control—in reverse. Kyle was so surprised he spun out.

Andy skidded to a halt behind the starting line where the surprised Todd stood. He rolled down his window just as an earthquake *RRRRUMBLED* and shook the area, startling them both.

"Huh," said Todd. "You beat Kyle. . . and then there's an earthquake."

"I—I'm sure those two things have nothing to do with each other. See you at the Spree." Andy plucked the wad of cash from Todd's hand and drove off.

The Day of Triumph knew no bounds.

fourteen

Lynn was so busy corralling the kids that she didn't notice Andy was late. He put his years of speed showering to good use and got ready in a flash. And wonder of wonders, Andy found himself actually looking forward to the Sienna Spree. It was an interesting feeling.

One of his reasons for not liking the event was because it was a costume party and Andy always picked the wrong costume. Not wrong in the sense that he put whatever he had chosen on incorrectly, but more that his choice wasn't very good.

It was going to be different this year. He and Danny

had worn matching costumes the past couple of years and it had been fun. Emily wanted no part of it and Lynn always went as a Denver sports personality. This year, they had planned on going as a couple of Transformers but after their meeting with the Oorts, Danny said he wanted to go as them. It would be their little (giant) secret.

Andy thought it was a great idea. He spray-painted a pair of overalls green, adorned them with a few bangles, and used thin wire and crepe paper to create antennae. Andy let Danny wear a cap pistol with a holster on his outfit. His son had been quite taken with Pilot Kezzek and wanted to look cool. Finally, some green makeup for their hands and faces did the trick.

Andy slid several tie clips on one side of his shirt to mimic Oortian rank designations while Danny studied himself in the mirror. "Being aliens is cool," his son said.

Andy kneeled and adjusted his son's antennae, whispering, "Remember, we thought these up. We've never seen aliens." Andy shook his head from side to side as he emphasized *never*.

Danny mirrored the head shake, causing his antennae to jiggle. "Yup. We've never seen aliens."

Lynn's football player costume came complete with eye black, shoulder pads, and Peyton Manning's Denver Bronco jersey. Andy gave her a thumbs-up as she finished a telephone conversation. "Yes, I'll pass that on. Okay."

Emily frowned at her princess costume in the mirror. "Ugh. This is so lame. My costume was *way* better."

"Miley Cyrus in rehab is not a costume," Andy said. "A princess, that's a costume."

Lynn hung up the phone. "Mrs. Wu says the dry cleaning machine you fixed is getting stains out without pretreating. And Mister Wu swears it sewed a button back on."

Andy laughed nervously. "Ol' Mister Wu. What a kidder."

Emily asked, "What if I go as Miley but not in rehab?"

"No, and stop saying rehab," said Andy.

Lynn came over to Andy, straightening one of the faux Oortian bangles on his chest. "That's the sixth call today. To hear them, you're some kind of wonder inventor. The name Thomas Edison was thrown out by Cliff Stevens."

"Cliff is a history buff," Andy said. He couldn't keep a proud smile from creeping onto his face as he made another adjustment to Danny's antennae. "And it does say *Handy* Andy on my truck."

Danny stopped his father from tweaking his costume. "It's good now, cool. Who's Thomas Edison?"

"He was a great inventor," said Andy.

Lynn tapped his shoulder. "Really. What's going on?"

She asked the question as seriously as you could while wearing eye black and a Peyton Manning jersey—taken in to look *cute*, of course.

Danny remained focused on Thomas Edison as he tugged on Andy's pants. "Did he invent Game Boy?"

"No. The light bulb and loads of other stuff."

Danny wasn't impressed. "Doesn't sound so great to me."

"What do you mean, what's going on?" Andy asked his wife. "You believe it's me whenever something goes wrong."

Emily rolled her eyes at her princess costume. "Can I just meet you guys later? Gina's mom can drive me."

"Gina, who thought up Miley in rehab? Didn't you hear? Oh you couldn't have, because she's grounded in her room with no computer or phone privileges for two weeks," Lynn said matter-of-factly, turning from Andy to her daughter. "It seems she was planning a party tonight."

Emily froze for a moment and then adjusted the intricate bow in her hair. "Really? Whoa. Must be something she was working on by herself and didn't tell me about. You know what? This costume doesn't look half bad. I think we should take a nice family picture at the Spree."

Lynn gave her daughter a peck on the cheek. "Very good answer. That's why you're my favorite daughter." She motioned to Andy and Danny. "How about we take this show on the road?"

Danny was ready and shouted, "Yay!"

The beam from the Oort ship sizzled into the ground, turning the area below it to molten slag and vapor. Kezzek checked the progress, nodding to himself. Lorel and Jarem clipped and bagged samples nearby. Leader Kolgan was in the process of having a formal picture taken in front of the spaceship. He posed with one hand in his uniform coat as the beam did its work in the background, unknowingly doing a great alien Napoleon impression.

Sub-Leader Nox peered into a sleek, but bulkier, camera set on a tripod. "That's it. Work it, work it," Nox said. "Give me a little more, 'I am the lord of all I survey, so deal with it.' Oh yes, simply majestic. If I may say, Leader Kolgan, my favorite part of each peace mission is taking your official portrait."

Kolgan nodded. "You may say that. Now take the picture. And make sure my eyes aren't closed like last time." The camera flashed an instant after the searing beam from the underside of the Oort ship turned off. When the two Oorts looked at Kezzek, he gave them a thumbs-up. Kolgan hopped off the stump. "Tell me you got the picture while the cutting laser was drilling the guide hole. You did, right? Let me see."

Nox evaded Kolgan's grasping hands. "Not this sub-second." Nox packed the camera and tripod up. "Of course I got it, with the beam lighting one half of your face.

It's magnificent. But before you see it I do need to make sure you don't have cerulean-eye and digitally smooth any fur tangles left from your exertions on this extremely hard peace mission. Only then will it be ready."

Kezzek came over to the pair. "Leader, the guide hole is complete. Is there time for a nap before the next stage of the mission?"

"What? No." Kolgan shooed the pilot away and yelled at his senior scientist. "Jarem, finish up. And tell Ron'nerlkjsdhfyerhfjlkejetc to heat my bath. I do like a warm bath after a successful peace mission."

"Go deal with that, please." Jarem motioned at Lorel. "It's a shame we can't stay a bit longer," he said to the Oort Leader. "Planet Dirt has a wide variety of flora and fauna."

"Scientists, always puttering," Kolgan said to Nox with a grin.

"They are so stupid," the Sub-Leader said.

Lorel came out of the ship and bowed to Kolgan. "Leader, Ron'nerlkjsdhfyerhfjlkejetc is not aboard the craft. Also, I think Pilot Kezzek's nap idea has merit."

Nox nodded. "I, for one, say good riddance."

"Oh, is that what you think?" Kolgan gave the Sub-Leader a slap to the back of the head. "The question you should be asking is where did he go, and why?"

"Junior Science Officer," Jarem said. "Scan for Yoglian DNA."

Lorel checked her computer pad, pressing a few buttons. "The signal is weak. It seems to be headed to the primitive gathering the Dirtlings are having on this day. The. . ." Lorel checked her pad. "Sienna Spree."

Jarem nodded. "Yes. Dirtling Andy mentioned attending that with its mate and spawn."

Kolgan purred and rubbed his furry chin. "His mate is going? The hot one? Interesting. Where exactly is this Sienna Spree occurring?"

Andy and family walked under an archway with a "Sienna Spree" sign. The park was decorated with balloons and streamers and at least half of the folks in attendance were in costume. Smaller kids played in the inflatable castle and ball pit. A long wooden bar that sold beer and wine stood on one side, while the other had all sorts of small town food classics like brisket, barbeque, chicken wings, and a dozen types of pie.

Andy bought strips of tickets as Danny jumped up and down with his hands out. "Tickets, tickets, tickets!"

"Be careful and no rough stuff in the ball pit." Andy handed Danny a wad of tickets and watched as his son took off.

Emily saw some of her friends and held out a disinterested hand. "Lame. But I guess I'll take a few." Andy gave his daughter her share.

Lynn put a warning hand on Emily's shoulder before she could disappear. "Stay around the main area. No sneaking off." Emily harrumphed and joined her friends.

Foreman Hank from A&S Machining—dressed as Harry Potter—wrapped Andy in a hug. "You're a genius. The air conditioner uses practically no electricity. By my calculations we'll save so much money we can buy new softball uniforms. And gloves." Hank shook Andy's hand—a lot—before he left.

Lynn looked at him suspiciously. "You want wine?" he asked. "I'll get wine."

Andy went out of his way to pass close to Kyle, standing with the Mister Fixx-It guys, as he walked to the bar. Kyle wore a lion costume while Ricky and Doug were green and blue M&Ms. "How's it going, Kyle? If you want to race again, I can use Emily's bike to make it more even."

Todd, Ricky, and Doug laughed. Andy did a double take when Todd walked past in an incredibly authentic Viking costume with helmet, blond braids, and a fake beard.

"Please vote for me for best costume, Andy," Todd said, waving his ax around.

Andy went to the bar. He surveyed the townspeople, his wife talking with a neighbor, Danny jumping in the ball pit, and Emily gossiping with friends. He sighed, content. He hoped that this day was the start of a new and wonderful chapter in their lives.

Andy raised a hand to attract a bartender when tentacles wrapped around his mouth and midsection and jerked him out of his reverie. He was pulled into the trees behind the bar. Ron wrapped him in four tentacles with a fifth still firmly over his mouth. He still had plenty left over to stand on. Andy struggled to no avail as his arms were pinned and his feet were completely off the ground.

Ron brought Andy close to his creepy maw of a mouth. "I must speak at you. Make a gesture if you comprehend." The terrified Andy nodded. Ron paused. "This is awkward. I do not fully understand human gestures. Was that a sign of agreement, or a bodily twitch?"

Ron moved the tentacle covering his mouth so he could speak. Andy spit several times afterward. "Oh, you got slime in my mouth. Yes, I'm agreeing, agreeing. Yuck."

Ron lowered Andy but kept a firm grip on his midsection and legs. "I need you to construct a bomblet to destroy the Oort space saucer," he said.

"A bomb? Are you crazy? I'm not making you a bomb." Before Andy could raise his voice to yell, Ron squeezed his midsection. Andy's "Help" came out as a breathy whisper.

Ron shook him in irritation. "Surely a few days with the Oort tool cannot be worth your planet? What else have they promised you?"

Andy was confused. "What do you mean? They didn't promise me anything."

Ron lowered him to the ground. "You do not betray your world for gain? Then why imitate an Oort?"

Andy pointed out others at the Spree who also had dressed up. "It's a costume party. Everyone does it and I just picked this." Ron's tentacles fell away. He bobbed his body in confusion as Andy wiped his face and tongue with a hankie.

"If you do not receive anything, and do not hate your world, why would you help destroy it?" Ron asked.

Andy stopped cleaning his tongue mid-wipe. "Destroy what now?"

Ron waved a few of his thinner tentacles around. "The Oorts eliminate any world with sentient life as it might threaten them in the future. That is their version of maintaining peace. They are, how to describe in your words. . . psychotic xenophobes. The Oorts are here to *destroy* your planet."

fifteen

A variety of feelings flashed through Andy after Ron told him that the Oorts were here to destroy the Earth; fear, disbelief, suspicion. Mostly disbelief. He worked to form a serious and intelligent question about the fuzzy, adorable Oorts being genocidal maniacs but could only come up with: "Are you joking?"

Ron bobbed his body. "Humor? Negative. The situation is not funny unless you are disturbed."

Andy shook his head. "This—you, are ridiculous. I—I—how can I trust you? Why would you help me—us?"

Ron's tentacles slumped. "I would do it as penance. I was a prince on my world. When the Oorts came, I convinced our king to reason with them instead of fight. It did not work. They destroyed my world." Ron started a high-pitched keening, swaying from side to side, and drooling from his weird maw. Andy realized it might be his race's version of crying.

He patted Ron's nearest tentacle. "Aww, I—I, umm—there, there." Ron swept Andy off his feet with a dozen tentacles in a crushing hug. The alien's high-pitched keening became louder and he leaked considerably more goo. "Oh God, let it out. Gross, you're literally letting it out. . . *eww*."

Ron's bulbous eyes widened and he pointed with a free tentacle. "They're here." Andy saw the Oorts march into the park. Kolgan led with Nox, Jarem, Lorel, and Kezzek following in their usual pecking order. Ron shook Andy by the shoulders. "I cannot word-fight with you any longer. Give me the Oort tool."

Ron's shaking made it difficult to respond. "It's—in—my—truck."

Ron wrapped a tentacle around his waist and shoved him forward. He squatted low to the ground and scuttled sideways, keeping the Oorts in view.

The townspeople applauded the Oorts, who to them, were kids dressed in great costumes. Kyle, Ricky, and Doug watched as an annoyed Todd plucked at his Viking beard. "They'll probably split votes for best costume since there's a bunch of 'em, right? I can still win. Shoot, I got my hair braided for this."

Kolgan waved, soaking up the applause. "These Dirtlings aren't entirely stupid. They recognize my greatness."

"Of course they do," said Sub-Leader Nox.

Kolgan nodded. "Excellent point."

Jarem held out his pad device, taking readings. On its screen he monitored a view from Andy's earring-tracker, complete with real time video of Ron pushing him along. "Keep yourself in motion," said Ron from the speaker on the pad as it fuzzed in and out.

"I'm trying," Andy said.

Jarem motioned to Lorel and Kezzek. "I'm getting a lot of interference and everything looks the same," said the Senior Scientist. "Search the area. Try that way first." The two Oorts peeled off from the group.

Andy's feet barely touched the ground as Ron shuttled him toward his truck. "Do you have components for a bomblet in your vehicle?"

"No, Ron. I don't keep bomb making equipment anywhere."

Ron gurgled in his language, frustrated. "If you don't care for your planet, don't you at least have feelings for your mate?"

"My mate?" Andy looked in the direction of Lynn. Leader Kolgan bowed before her. Jarem and Nox stood behind him.

"Kolgan has an unhealthy fixation on her. Now, where is the tool?" Ron asked.

Andy motioned with his chin. "It's in my toolbox. Let me go and I promise I'll give it to you." Ron let him loose. Andy climbed into the pickup, paused by his toolbox, and then dove out the other side, slamming the door on Ron's grasping tentacles.

Andy grabbed the Oort tool from his pocket. "Put this in your pouch and smoke it!" He whipped the tool over Ron's head and ran to Lynn.

"Wait," said Ron. "What does that even mean?"

Most of the people attending the Sienna Spree were gathered around Lynn, Leader Kolgan, Sub-Leader Nox, and Senior Scientist Jarem. Kyle, Todd, Ricky, Doug, Mister and Mrs. Wu, Principal Brennan, Hank the machine shop foreman, Sheriff Ralston, and young Deputy Bob all watched the scene as Lynn spoke with the Oorts.

"Your costumes are so cute," she said. She rubbed Kolgan's head and he blushed, turning crimson for a moment. Literally. The crowd *ohhhhh-ed* this change of color.

"Oh, come on," said Todd.

Leader Kolgan's color changed back to his usual light green. "Oh, that's the stuff. I'm glad you approve, because I'm taking you with me as my new Dancing Queen."

Sub-Leader Nox leaned in to Lynn and said, "You should be very proud."

Andy pushed his way through the crowd and grabbed his wife's hand. "Getting kinda late, don't you think, honey? We should get the kids home."

Lynn remained playfully deferential to Kolgan. "I don't think we can. After all, I've just been named Dancing Queen."

Andy tugged her hand as the crowd laughed. "Very nice, time to go."

Leader Kolgan wasn't keen on this interruption. "Let go of my Dancing Queen, Dirtling. Nox, restrain her."

The Sub-Leader grabbed Lynn's leg. She tried to shake him off but Nox hung on tight. "Oh, hello. You're getting a little hands-y," she said.

The crowd gasped as Andy was lifted from the ground by Ron. "Andy, I beseech your help."

Todd threw his Viking axe onto the ground. "Oh,

come on, that's gotta be store-bought. Homemade costumes only! I call rules violation!"

Leader Kolgan and Jarem stood on one side with Nox, who was still clutching Lynn's leg. Ron had a couple of tentacles wrapped around Andy's waist, tugging at him while he continued to pull Lynn.

"Kolgan, is it true?" Andy asked. "Are you here to destroy Earth?"

Kolgan considered this and then addressed the gathered crowd. "I will speak now."

Nox shushed everyone, slapping their knees whether they were speaking or not. "Quiet! Our illustrious Leader will now speak. Shut your juice drains!" This got a big chuckle from everyone.

Kolgan hopped onto a picnic table and addressed the crowd. "Our satellites detected your planet some time ago. As is our way, we flew across the great galaxy on a mission of peace." The crowd murmured appreciatively. "During our journey a terrible meteor storm damaged our ship and forced us to crash land. The situation was dire. If it weren't for my insanely excellent leadership, we would have died."

Jarem sighed and rolled his eyes at this. Kolgan continued. "We crashed on your planet. We were helpless, our mission in jeopardy. But one among you, the Dirtling Andy, repaired our ship." The crowd gave Andy a good-natured round of applause. Lynn kissed him theatrically on the cheek. "So now we can lift off and ensure peace between our races forever. . . by blowing your planet to smithereens."

Silence from the crowd. Some had their hands frozen in a clapping position.

"Excuse me, what was that last part?" asked Sheriff Ralston, dressed as a London bobby.

Kolgan faced Ralston, giving him an imperious glare. "We're here to destroy your planet. How else can we maintain peace?"

Mrs. Wu, joined at the hip with Mister Wu in a Siamese twin costume, elbowed her husband. "Aww, he's so crazy and cute."

Leader Kolgan pointed at Andy. "Once more, I thank you, Dirtling Andy. We would have had no chance of destroying your planet without your considerable help." Everyone turned to Andy. "By the way, you're coming with us," the Oort continued. "There might be another meteor storm. And you shall inform me of my Dancing Queen's likes and dislikes." Kolgan drew his ray gun and aimed it at Andy and Lynn.

"Hold on, Kolgan," Andy said. "Let's talk about this."

"I'll save you, Lynn," said Ricky, in his green M&M costume. He stepped in front of Kolgan. "This looks like a job for a chocolaty hero."

The Oort leader zapped Ricky, who fell to the ground, twitching.

The crowd was silent until Todd punched a fist into the air. "Awesome! Do Doug next."

"Now wait a—" was what Doug got out before Kolgan shrugged and fired.

ZAAAAP!

Doug joined Ricky on the ground. Kolgan holstered his weapon and motioned to his Sub-Leader. "Bring them."

Before Nox could draw his gun, a tentacle tapped his shoulder, distracting him. Another tentacle grabbed the gun from his holster and flung it away.

Ron placed himself between Andy and Lynn and the Sub-Leader. The Oort stared at Ron with loathing. "Oh no, you didn't. I know you didn't just grab my gat."

Ron shoved Nox's little chest with one tentacle and moved Andy and Lynn behind him with a couple of others. "I believe I did, buttock-hole. What will you do about it?"

With an angry purr, Nox sprang at Ron, who snatched the Oort from the air and slammed him on the ground several times—left, right, left, right. Nox managed to bite the tentacle holding him, causing Ron to yank it away. He sucked on his injured appendage with his maw. "You bit me."

Nox kicked a picnic table plank free. He waved this

makeshift club easily, being far stronger than the cuddly toy he resembled. "A small down payment on the Sub-Leader style beatdown you shall now receive, Squid Face."

Off to the side, Senior Scientist Jarem drew his ray gun and took aim at Ron. Kolgan stopped him with a raised hand. "Hold. I kind of want to see this."

The little Oort and the far larger Ron circled each other. Some in the crowd thought it was a show, others were confused. They moved to give Ron and Nox space.

The two had never liked each other and in a flash were going at it full bore. For the lucky viewers of the first extraterrestrial fight to ever occur on Earth, it was a mix of the Three Stooges and Bugs Bunny. The crowd *ooohed*, *ahhhed*, and laughed as the hits kept coming.

Andy took the opportunity to spirit Lynn away. "We've got to find the kids and get out of here," he said.

sixteen

Pilot Kezzek and Junior Science Office Lorel were into the booze at the empty bar. Kezzek chugged a beer, smacking his lips. "This stuff makes me feel *fun-kaay*."

Lorel took a drink from a bottle of wine, stumbling sideways. "Yes. It makes me want to do questionable things."

Kezzek heard the roar from the crowd. He moved so he could see the fight between Ron and Nox. "Hit him in the *jarkles* for me, Ron'nerlkjsdhfyerhfjlkejetc!"

Lorel liked this. "You're such a bad boy."

Kezzek grinned, drank the rest of his beer, and let

out a mighty burp.

Lorel purred and tackled him.

Ron gained the upper hand in the fight. Nox couldn't fend off the attacking tentacles coming from every direction; left, right, high, low, even from behind. "I believe on this planet this is called opening a can of whoop sass," Ron said.

Off to the side, Leader Kolgan handed Jarem a brightly colored bill. "Looks like you win," he said. After putting the bill into his pocket, Jarem sprang into the air, looping several times. He landed perfectly on a picnic table with his gun drawn and fired at Ron.

FZZZZZTT!

Ron's tentacles jerked in different directions. He fell onto a table, crushing it flat.

Sheriff Ralston stepped forward, waving the night stick from his London bobby costume. "Okay, this show of yours is getting too darn violent. Put those guns down. Now."

Kolgan glanced at Jarem. "Double or nothing for most Dirtlings *gazoortzed*?"

"In some of the words of the Dirtlings, 'It's on like Donkey Kong.'" Both Oorts drew their ray guns and fired at the surrounding townspeople.

Everyone panicked, running in all directions. Down went Mister Wu, a couple of Hank's A&S Machining workers, and Principal Brennan. Ralston dodged and weaved like a man who had been under fire previously in his life, before flopping behind an overturned picnic table. His petrified deputy was already there, scared out of his wits.

Ralston grabbed him by the collar. "Private, find 25-Set and confirm VC contact two clicks south of firebase. Call in the Jolly Greens for dust off and evac!"

Deputy Bob ducked low when a ray gun blast hit nearby. "Sheriff, what the heck are you talking about?"

Danny and Emily climbed into the back seat of the pickup. Andy tried to push Lynn in the driver's side, but she wouldn't get in. "So those are *real* aliens? Really real aliens?"

"Yes, Lynn. Really real aliens."

"Daddy fixed their spaceship," Danny said.

Andy threw the antennae from his costume away and wiped his face of green makeup. "We'll talk later. Right now you have to go hide."

"In the middle of the night? Where?"

Andy pointed at the driver's seat. "Lynn! Get in the darn truck," he yelled. His wife reluctantly slid inside.

"Andy! What the hell is going on?" Kyle asked as he ran over, still wearing his cowardly lion costume. "Those costumed idiots destroyed the buffet. *Before* I got to eat. This is—"

Kyle fell silent as the brightly colored Oort ship drifted across the park just thirty feet off the ground. The spaceship settled over Andy's truck, emitting its odd moaning noise as its scales rippled, changing color.

Townspeople stared from behind trees and on the ground. Hiding underneath a picnic table, Hank the Foreman sipped a can of beer with a couple of his machine shop workers, all in their various costumes. "Boy, Spree committee really went all out this year."

Leader Kolgan and Nox joined Andy as the ship stopped overhead. The Sub-Leader used his remote control to put it in hover. "Where is Pilot Kezzek? He should be doing this."

Jarem threw his hands out, disgusted. "And my Junior Science Officer is nowhere to be found, either. I shall search for them both."

"Dirtling Andy, there is no need for craziness," Kolgan said. "In my magnificent wisdom, I have decided your entire family unit can come with us."

Emily and Danny got out of the truck and clung to Andy with Lynn.

"What does he mean, Dad?" asked Emily.

Andy shook his head. "Leave them be. I'll go."

Leader Kolgan puffed his chest out, hands on his hips. "You dare question me? I think not. Your mate will be my Dancing Queen. Jarem will display your spawn in the Oortian Museum of Freaks, and you will be my ever-shamed menial laborer. Done and done."

Sub-Leader Nox leaned in toward Andy and his family. "See? It's all good."

Jarem guided the very drunk Lorel to the gathering as Kezzek dragged a hog-tied Ron by a couple of his tentacles. "I don't feel so hot." Kezzek vomited a Technicolor yawn. Could alien upchucking be cute? Apparently, yes. "Sooo much better," the pilot said.

Lorel fell sideways and did the same. Jarem waved his furry hands in frustration. "For the love of science, pull yourselves together."

Kyle had had enough. "That's it. Playtime is *over*. You kids are in big, big trouble. When I—" Kolgan gave a disinterested hand signal to Nox, who shot Kyle. He snorted once and tumbled onto the ground.

"Oh my God," said Lynn. She checked on her brother, who groaned.

Nox pressed a button and a blue ray emanated from the ship. Lynn, Kyle, Emily, and Danny were caught in the beam and lifted upwards. Kezzek threw Ron into the blue light and stepped in it himself. Jarem, Lorel, and Nox did likewise. The craft's underside bay opened to receive everyone. The kids yelled in fright. "Andy," Lynn said. "Do something."

Andy stood outside of the beam and turned to Kolgan, frantic. "Stop it. You're scaring them."

The Oort leader laughed. "Then you should come and calm them down. And don't forget your tools."

Andy's shoulders slumped. He picked up his toolbox and stepped into the light after Kolgan. Both were elevated into the bay, which closed after they were inside. Then the ship accelerated into the night sky and out of sight.

The townspeople came out of hiding and gathered in a cluster to watch the receding spaceship. Those that were hit by the ray guns shakily got to their feet. After a moment, Mrs. Wu clapped. "Best Sienna Spree ever."

seventeen

Kolgan and Jarem walked behind Andy, Lynn, Kyle, Emily, and Danny. The adults had to lean their heads to varying degrees, but at least the kids fit in the hallway all right. Ron scrunched down and glided along on his tentacles, none the worse for wear. Limping noticeably, Nox covered the group with his ray gun. Kezzek did the same.

Lorel took several pictures as the humans walked. When she scanned Danny with her computer pad, Emily grabbed the device and flung it down the corridor. "Leave my brother alone, you alien booger," she said.

"Ha!" said Danny. "Alien booger. Because you're green."

Lorel gave a little *hmph* and went after the pad.

Andy carried his toolbox with one hand and his woozy brother in law with the other. Lynn also helped prop up Kyle as he regained his senses. "What happened? Where are we?"

"Do you remember when I told you I saw aliens in the woods?" asked Andy

"I don't see what the immigration issue has to do with this," said Kyle.

Andy gestured at their captors. Realization dawned on Kyle. His eyes darted to each of the Oorts and Ron. ". . . Oh, oh, oh! They're real aliens? How can there be aliens? No way, no way."

Lorel and Nox encased everyone in a translucent force field from their ray guns, similar to the one that had lifted them into the ship's bay. This bluish energy formed a bubble extending to the ground.

"Put the Dirtlings in a cell," said Kolgan, who then pointed at Lynn. "Except for you, my delicate rose. You shall live in my spare cabin."

"Another great honor," the Sub-Leader said. "What a day it's been for you."

Nox separated Lynn from the others despite her pounding on the barrier. "Let me out of here! Don't worry kids! Everything will be fine!" They pushed her down a different corridor, followed by Kolgan and Kezzek.

Andy kicked and punched the force bubble. "Lynn, I'll get you out. I promise!"

Lorel floated Andy, Kyle, and the kids to the far end of a bare room. Jarem stopped her from shutting the force field off. "One moment." The Senior Scientist used his ray gun and zapped the toolbox. Andy tried to hold onto it, but the field from Jarem's gun pushed his hands away. When the toolbox was next to Jarem, Lorel shut off her ray. A clear barrier came down from the ceiling before Andy could spring at the two Oorts. He pounded against the divider. "Let us out of here." The Oorts ignored him, comparing data on their pads.

Behind Andy, Ron gurgled in the corner, dropping bits of goo.

"Gross," said Emily.

Kyle grabbed Danny and Emily, pressing their heads melodramatically into his chest. "Nothing to worry about, kids. There's no slimy squid monster and we're not in an alien prison. Let's close our eyes and think of nice things like unicorns and fluffy clouds." He sang in a shaky whisper. "Twinkle, twinkle, little star, how I wonder where you are. . ."

Danny and Emily were more curious than scared of Ron. He lifted a tentacle in greeting and the kids waved back. "Hi," said Danny as his sister looked on.

Jarem and Lorel conferred with each other, talking

low as they tapped away on their alien pads. "They seem agitated and/or afraid." Lorel said.

Jarem purred in agreement. "I believe you're right. Perhaps a familiar setting will soothe them."

Andy stopped pounding on the barrier when the room morphed into an ultra-real ocean environment with coral, seaweed, and fish swimming around them. Though there was no water, Kyle grabbed his neck as if he were drowning. "Can't breathe. . . "

"I don't believe Dirtlings live underwater," said Jarem. "Try again."

Lorel pressed another button. Now the captives were on a tropical island—with a volcano erupting in the background. Kyle ran in a circle, flailing his arms. Andy hugged Danny and Emily while Ron just stood there.

"Lava! Hot lava! We're all going to die!" Kyle shouted.

Scientist Jarem shook his head. "Perhaps something less loud."

Lorel tried again. The room morphed into an aviary full of small, chirping birds. Andy, Kyle, and the kids calmed. A parakeet landed on Ron. His tentacles jerked and twitched. "Get it off, get it off, get it off!" he said in gurgling shriek as he twirled in a circle, scaring the humans.

Jarem gave Lorel a disapproving purr.

"Ah, what am I doing? We have images of Dirtling

Andy's own lair," she said.

Click.

The cell morphed into the kids' room, complete with masking tape line down the center. Ron stopped spinning and flailing. "I am extremely embarrassed and ashamed at my behavior."

Emily hopped onto her bed. She saw Danny was scared and motioned for him to sit by her side. He joined his sister on the bed. "You can be on my side," she said. "But only because we're on an alien spaceship."

"I know," Danny said. "I'm not dumb."

"Let's see if we can't get you de-greened," Emily said. She ripped a piece of her princess costume off and wiped Danny's face with it.

Jarem nodded in satisfaction. "See? Already adapting."

Andy went to the barrier nearest to the Oorts. "Jarem, Lorel. You're on a peace mission, but you're going to destroy our planet? That doesn't make any sense."

"Of course it does," said Jarem. They could hear each other perfectly through the barrier. Lorel flicked on a wall monitor. A beautiful orange planet came on the screen. "Here is our last peace mission to Tovalan. The Tovals had intricate neck sacs and could make the most beautiful trilling music." Andy watched the monitor as a huge laser cannon slid into view. It was the gun barrel point of view from the bay of the Oort ship.

Jarem and Lorel stood on either side of the monitor as a green beam fired from the cannon. "Remember how the Tovals serenaded the rising and setting of their twin suns, Senior Scientist?"

Jarem purred. "Yes. Delightful."

Far below, the beam hit the orange planet. Andy watched in horror as that world boiled and then crumbled into pieces. "My God, you're insane. Jarem—all those people. How could you do that? You're a scientist."

Jarem crossed his arms, irritated. "Destroying worlds before they become a threat makes us safer and preserves peace. The science is settled on this." He motioned for Lorel to follow and they walked out the room. "I doubt your primitive Dirtling brain can understand our advanced logic. Now try to make yourselves at home. Lorel and I must get a few more pictures of your planet before we blow it up."

The Junior Scientist purred. "And then we won't have to speak Dirtling anymore. But still, it's not as bad as Tovalese." Lorel trilled as Jarem chuckled at the memory.

Andy stared helplessly as the Oorts left, the door locking behind them with a click.

eighteen

Lynn had been locked on one side of Leader Kolgan's private room. She caught a reflection of herself and vigorously rubbed away the eye black of her costume. The room was divided in two by a clear barrier meant to keep her on that side. The other was opulently decorated with divans, cushions, and low tables.

Nox came in and sat down on the furnished side in a recliner with a control pad built into the armrest. "Still here?" he asked with a grin. "That was a great joke by me."

Lynn slapped the barrier. "Let me out of here, you little—whatever you are."

Nox ignored her and pressed a control button. A drawer slid out from the wall on Lynn's side. "I do not listen to Dirtlings. You listen to me. Put on the Dancing Queen uniform."

"You really think I'm going to wear that?" Lynn asked. "You're dumber than you look."

Nox purred in irritation. "Incorrect. Yes, you will." His furry finger stabbed another button. A light mist descended from the ceiling and cleared almost immediately.

"No, you listen to me—" When Lynn raised her arm to hit the barrier again, the sleeve of her Broncos uniform broke off and shattered on the floor. Her clothing was petrified. The more she moved, the more crackled away. "What's going on? Stop it. Oh!" Lynn grabbed the outfit from the tray as the remaining shards of her uniform fell off. She used the tiny costume to cover herself and stared daggers at the Sub-Leader.

Nox blanched and averted his eyes. "Eww, how many orifices do you Dirtlings have? You should inform Leader Kolgan which one does what. A good Dancing Queen would do that."

"Get out of here, you little pervert."

"With extreme pleasure," Nox said. He got up from the recliner. "I'm going to have nightmares."

Andy took a running start and double-kicked the barrier imprisoning them. He landed on the floor hard. Danny and Emily went over to him, worried.

"You okay?" asked Danny.

"Sure thing, kiddo."

"Are you done?" his brother in law asked. "Is ten times enough?" Kyle kept his distance from Ron, eyeing him from time to time.

Andy pressed his face against the barrier and stared longingly at his toolbox. It was only a few feet away, but might as well have been on the moon. He sighed, sitting down and putting his hands on his head.

Emily patted him on the shoulder. "It's going to be okay, Dad."

Danny agreed. "Yeah, you'll find a way to save us. We know you will."

Andy got up and tousled his son's hair. "Thanks, son."

"Do you have a plan, maybe?" asked Kyle.

"If I could just get my tools."

"Would the Oort tool be of use?" Ron asked.

Andy whirled. "You still have it?"

"I stuck it in my pouch as you told me to do, but I did not smoke it. I apologize." Ron brought out the tool from his pouch with a tentacle. It emerged dripping slime.

Emily blanched. "That's super gross."

"Super gross or not, it's the most important thing in

the world to us right now, kiddo." Andy wiped the baton on his shirt, aimed it at the barrier, and then pressed the button. Nothing happened. He began pacing back and forth. "Nothing's broken. It won't work if nothing's broken."

Emily picked up the lamp on her desk and smashed it. The pieces disappeared from the floor, but the lamp reappeared on the desk like new.

"Cool!" said Danny.

Andy frowned. "No Danny, not cool. We need to break something not created by the room. Something it can't replace." He rubbed his face, thinking, and his hand brushed the alien earring.

Bingo!

"Ron, can you hit my ear tracker so it breaks?" Andy asked, holding out the Oort tool.

Ron took the baton, wrapping a smaller tentacle around it. "I believe so."

Andy went to his hands and knees and put his head on the floor, stretching his ear lobe as far as it would go. He took a couple of steadying breaths and said, "Okay, do it."

Ron held Andy's shoulders down with a couple thick tentacles. He splayed himself out for more leverage, which made him look very spidery and a little creepy—like he was going to eat Andy.

Emily couldn't help herself and shrieked at the scene.

This frightened Kyle and Danny so much that they joined in, not knowing why they were screaming. Kyle's scream was not only loudest, but highest-pitched.

This startled Ron as he swung the tool, causing him to miss the Oort earring and solidly connect with Andy's head. Andy, in turn, howled like a banshee. Ron added his own gurgling cries to the mix as he twirled and flailed his tentacles. This caused Kyle and the kids to yell even louder.

It was chaos in their alien prison cell as Andy struggled to his knees, woozy from the blow to his head. "Everyone stop. Quiet." The group calmed. Andy pointed at Ron, who shifted from tentacle to tentacle in an embarrassed way. "I said, 'Hit the earring,' not my head."

Ron keened, swaying from side to side. "I am useless and unworthy. You cannot expect me to do anything correctly."

Andy rubbed Ron on the back of his bulbous head. "Hey, it's okay. Without you, we wouldn't have known about the Oort's plans until it was too late. And it's not too late. But I need your help now."

"Thank you for those words," Ron said. "I will try, but please take your hand off my *garrrrk'nix*. You are making me extremely not-comfortable."

Andy pulled his hand away, wiping it on his shirt. He got down on the floor once more. "Kids, shut your eyes this time. Kyle, no yelling."

Emily and Danny closed their eyes. Kyle, not trusting himself, put a hand over his mouth. Andy nodded and Ron smashed down on the earring. This time it popped off. Andy jumped up and down as he massaged his ear. "Whoa, that was painful. But I'm okay, you can open your eyes, kids. Dad's okay. Ron, the tool." He handed Andy the Oort baton. "When I press the button do not—repeat, do *not*—let the tool fix the earring. We grab those heads and use them on the barrier. Steady now. Here we go."

Andy pointed the baton at the smashed earring and pressed the button. The Oort tool formed different heads; one held the earring in place, another disassembled it, a third put the pieces neatly in order, a fourth made itself into a tiny, powerful torch.

It was a good thing Ron had so many tentacles. Only he could have wrestled the various appendages of the Oort device, which twisted like snakes, trying to do their work. Andy stepped backwards, making the appendages even longer. "Grab the handle, Kyle."

His brother-in-law shook his head. "I don't think so."

"Yes. Do it now," Andy ordered.

Kyle grabbed the baton handle and took Andy's place. He hopped from foot to foot, scared out of his wits. "Satan tool. Satan tool."

Andy grabbed the torch. It took all of his strength, but

he managed to point it at the barrier. "Little help, Ron. Push. Almost. . . " With an assist from one of Ron's free tentacles, Andy used the torch to cut an opening in the barrier wall.

On Kyle's end, the Oort tool sparked and smoked. "Hurry. I think it's gonna blow."

"Little more, little more," Andy said. He finished cutting and watched an oval-shaped section of the barrier fall away. Kyle threw the baton into the corner. It frenetically twisted, looped into itself, then shorted out. The tool didn't revert to its compact baton form. It just laid there, dead.

"We broke it," Andy said with a tinge of sadness.

His son interrupted this reverie. "Daddy, I wanna go home."

Kyle nodded. "Me too. What now?"

Andy turned to Ron. "Is there an escape pod on this ship?"

The alien gave a confused bob of his body. "Yes, but why would that help?" Kyle, Emily, and Danny looked at Ron the way you would expect.

Andy didn't have time to be annoyed. "It just would."

"I will show you then." Ron hauled himself through the hole in the barrier and everyone else followed.

nineteen

Andy, Kyle, Emily, Danny, and Ron crept their way down the spaceship corridor. Oort voices echoed from the bridge and Andy motioned for everyone to press against the wall. Thankfully, the voices moved off.

"How much farther?" Andy whispered to Ron.

Ron scuttled—it seemed when he was tense or nervous he more scuttled than glided—thirty feet down the hallway and opened a hatch. The escape pod was small but had enough room for their purposes. Andy nodded. "Okay, good. Everyone inside."

After making sure the kids were safely inside, Ron

folded himself into the pod, clinging to the low ceiling. When Andy motioned for Kyle to enter, he shook his head. "Nope, nope, nope. No way."

"Oh, come on," Andy said. "Ron's a really nice. . . being. There's nothing to be afraid of."

"Who's afraid? This escape pod is full." Andy tried pushing, but Kyle used his hands and feet to stay outside. "I'll follow in the next one. Besides, Lynn's still missing, so I'll have to kick some alien butt and get her."

"No. I want you to stay with the kids."

His brother in law turned to argue. "I think—"

Andy cut him off. "Get in the darn pod and watch the kids. Now."

Kyle shivered involuntarily when he looked at Ron. A dollop of slime dripped off the alien's bulbous head as he clung to the ceiling and wall. Kyle climbed inside the pod and wagged a finger at the alien. "Stay on that side."

Andy smiled at Danny and Emily with confidence he didn't really feel. "I'm going to get Mom. Stay and protect Uncle Kyle. Be back soon, I promise."

Andy was about to close the door when Kyle leaned over. "Andy. . . I—I want you to know. . . I'm a jerk."

"I already knew that," said Andy with a smile. "But you're family." He closed the door to the escape pod and jogged down the hallway.

Earth dominated the view screen on the bridge as Pilot Kezzek operated his controls. Senior and Junior Science Officers Jarem and Lorel were at their science stations taking readings. Leader Kolgan sat on his raised chair, relaxed and pleased with himself.

"We are in synchronous orbit over the guide hole, Leader," said Kezzek.

Sub-Leader Nox entered the bridge and took his lower seat at Kolgan's side. "Your Dancing Queen is dressed," he said.

"Everything's comin' up Kolgan." He purred in satisfaction. "Deploy the Peacemaker, Pilot."

Pilot Kezzek flipped switches at his station. "Rockin' and rollin', lockin' and loadin'."

The bay door opened on the underside of the Oort ship. An absolute beast of a laser cannon emerged from it, looking as out of place as a fluffy bunny with a bazooka. The cannon grew larger and larger as its many sections telescoped outward. Fully deployed, the Peacemaker was larger than the entire vessel. The monstrous gun tracked downward, taking aim at planet Earth. The entire bridge resounded with a deep *thunk* as the cannon locked into place.

"Your pickle is hot, sir," said Pilot Kezzek.

Leader Kolgan purred again, leaning back into his

chair. "The moment before the end of a successful mission is sweet. Jarem, are you finished?"

Jarem and Lorel pressed buttons and adjusted knobs on their control boards. "Calibrating sensors and recording devices for maximum resolution," Lorel said.

Jarem gave Leader Kolgan a little bow. "Very sorry. Just a few more minutes, Leader."

Kolgan frowned but allowed it. "You have the bridge," he told Nox. "But don't sit in my chair, or do anything without checking with me first." With that said, Kolgan left.

Nox preened and sat up straighter while giving Kezzek an I'm-better-than-you-are look. "That means my pickle is also hot," he said. "Yes, I have a very hot pickle indeed."

Kezzek rolled his eyes and got back to monitoring his station.

Lynn searched for a way out of Leader Kolgan's private room, but there was none. Her new costume consisted of a slinky top and a short, sarong-like bottom. It was colorful with tiny bells attached at the hips that made a melodic tinkling whenever she kicked the barrier.

The outer door opened and Andy snuck inside, closing it behind himself.

"Andy," she said, relieved. "Thank God."

He put his eye against a peephole in the door and made sure no one was coming down the corridor. It was clear, for the moment.

"The controls to the barrier are on that recliner." Lynn pointed.

Andy quickly sat and looked over the pad on the chair's arm. The first button he hit turned on the mood lighting. He tried another. Andy's chair zipped flat, turning into (for him) a mini-bed. It vibrated madly, causing him to tumble off. "Come on, already." Frustrated, Andy punched the console and the barrier disappeared.

He and Lynn flew into a hug. "Are you okay?" he asked.

"Yes, I'm so glad to see you."

Now that they were reunited, Andy noticed Lynn's Dancing Queen outfit. More than noticed. "Me, too, so glad," he said. "So glad."

Lynn chuckled. "Can you believe they made me put this on?"

Andy was mesmerized. He thought his wife looked stunning in the Oort costume. "Yes, horrible. I'll give them a. . . good talking to. For sure."

Lynn shook him by the shoulders. "Hey. We're prisoners on an alien spaceship that's about to destroy the Earth."

Andy snapped out of his stupor. "Right, momentary lapse. Let's go. Kids and Kyle are already in the escape pod." Andy led Lynn to the door and used the peephole to check the corridor. The big hat filling the lens made the approaching Oort Leader hard to miss. "Shoot. Kolgan's coming."

Andy grabbed one of the small tables and stood next to the door with it over his head.

"No, they're too fast. I'll dance for him." She pressed the button on the control chair and ran to the other side before it closed.

He didn't like this one bit. "There's no way you're doing that. Besides, I can take him."

Lynn slapped her hand on the barrier to get his attention. "I mean I'll distract him, then you can hit him. Now hide."

Andy put the table down, embarrassed. He dove behind a divan as the door opened and Kolgan entered. The Oort leader took off his hat, licking his palm to slick back the fur on his head before facing Lynn. "You look enchanting. And I have good news. I'm going to allow you to dance for me before *and* after I complete the peace mission and destroy your planet. How's that sound, my sweet, sweet Dancing Queen?"

"Sounds great. What's your name again?"

The Oort leader became petulant. "Leader Kolgan is my name. You *will* remember it." He let out a low purr. "But when we're alone, you shall call me. . . Big Boy."

On the floor, Andy gritted his teeth. It took all of his

self-control not to leap up and strangle the little green alien. Kolgan slapped a few buttons on the console chair, causing what looked very much like a disco ball to lower from the ceiling. Oortian music played, a weird and melodic mash of twittering harmonies. There was no real beat, so Lynn awkwardly swung her hips from side to side. The bells on her costume tinkled.

Kolgan loved it. "Yeah, that's the stuff."

"I'm so far away from you," Lynn said. "Couldn't you make this mean ol' divider go away—oh yuck—Big Boy?"

Kolgan purred and opened the barrier with a no-look button press. Lynn danced toward him, swaying and moving, trying to keep all of his attention on her. Andy rose behind him, slowly and silently, table in hand. Just then the Oort reclined his chair far enough to see Andy before he could strike.

Kolgan zipped to the side. "Oh-ho! Sedition and treason on your first day? You're a naughty, naughty Dancing Queen." The Oort bounced off a cushion—then the wall—and blasted apart the small table with his feet, leaving Andy holding one leg of the splintered furniture. "I'll prove my worth and then make beautiful *fnurtklk* at you, my sweet, sweet Dancing Queen."

Kolgan used the ping-ponging attack once more. This time Andy was ready and swung the leg of the table like a baseball bat, hitting him solidly.

"Nobody *fnurt-kliks* my wife but me," Andy said.

Kolgan sprung onto his feet with an angry purr. He ricocheted off the walls, the ceiling, the floor—punching Andy with his tiny fist each time he whizzed past. It looked ridiculous, but no two ways about it, Andy was getting badly beaten. He punched and kicked at Kolgan's speeding form but missed by a mile each time. "Run, Lynn . . . I'm good . . . I got this."

Andy managed to grab Kolgan on one pass. The two grappled. It was like fighting a cute stuffed animal—if cute stuffed animals had the speed of a cheetah and the strength of a gorilla. After one exceptionally solid hit, Andy fell onto his back.

Kolgan raised his furry little fist to deliver the *coup de grace*.

From behind him, Lynn said, "Hey, Big Boy. . . "

Kolgan whirled, but too late. She kicked him soccer-style to the other side of the room. The Oort hit the wall with a thud. Lynn pressed the button controlling the barrier and it came down, trapping the Oort leader.

She helped the shaky Andy to his feet. "If we ever get to tell this story. . . "

"You kicked his furry butt."

Kolgan rapped frantically on the barrier as Lynn and Andy dashed out of the room. "Don't leave me, my beautiful Dancing Queen. I looove you!"

twenty

Andy and Lynn kept their heads low as they ran down the corridor. "How much more time before they find out about Kolgan?" Lynn asked.

The corridor lit up, flashing red and yellow. A perky alarm went off, sounding like something from a video game.

"None," Andy said. He stripped off his green Oort shirt and tossed it to Lynn, who dressed as they ran. He skidded to a halt and yanked open the escape pod's hatch. Startled, Kyle banged his head on the ceiling. "Oww. For the love of Pete."

Emily and Danny hugged Lynn as she climbed inside. "Mom!"

His daughter saw the Oort outfit Lynn was wearing. "Oh, and my costume was bad?"

Lynn waggled her finger in a mock-serious way. "What have I told you about playing gotcha?" The three hugged once more. "I'm so glad to see you both."

Andy kneeled down and checked inside the now-even-more-cramped escape pod. "Okay, it's gonna be tight, but I think we can all fit."

Ron flattened himself onto the ceiling to make room as Andy got a leg in. "I must ask again, why is this good?"

Andy chuckled, relieved to have his family together. He didn't mind explaining. "Ron, this is an escape pod. So, we can use it to *escape*."

The alien bobbed his body in confusion. "But the pod can only be launched if the ship sustains so much damage that its destruction is imminent. Otherwise, why would one want to escape from a perfectly good ship?" Andy's face fell. Ron continued, "My kind has colonies not found by the Oorts. It's a long voyage, but your family would be safe. Provided the pod could be launched."

Andy motioned for Kyle to hand him his toolbox. He moved back out into the corridor. "This pod *will* launch. I guarantee it." He looked at his son and daughter. "I love you both so much."

"No, Dad," said Emily, as she began crying.

"Hey, I'll be right back," Andy said, trying to lighten the mood. "And I won't be a spaz."

Emily threw her arms around his neck. "I'm sorry I said that," she sobbed. "Please don't go. I've always been proud of you. And—and—secretly, I thought what happened at the science fair was hi-hi-hilarioussss." Emily wailed into his shoulder.

"It's okay," he said. "It's all right."

Danny's lip trembled. He turned to his mother. "Where's Daddy going? Is he not coming with us?"

"He's coming, don't worry," she said. Lynn wriggled from the escape pod to join him.

Andy faced his wife. "I have to try. I think you agree that it doesn't get any more big picture than this."

"I know," she said. Lynn kissed him and climbed back inside. "For luck."

Andy closed the door of the pod just as Sub-Leader Nox saw him. "Halt, Dirtling!" The Oort ran after him firing his ray gun. Andy ducked around a corner. After a few rapid turns he hid in a darkened recess. Nox rushed by without stopping.

Andy moved down the hall looking, looking—there!—he found a dumbwaiter opening like the one on the bridge. He stabbed the button next to it with his finger and the panel opened. Sure enough, there was a pole leading down to the engine room. Andy had managed to lift himself inside when he and his toolbox were encased in a bluish force field.

Nox levitated him into the corridor and closed the panel. "Like a Dirtling could ever outthink me," he said with a smirk.

Andy struggled uselessly as he was floated into the bridge area. Leader Kolgan, back in full uniform, scowled. "Disrupting a peace mission. Disrupting my Dancing Queen's inaugural dance. Have you no shame?"

Lorel herded Lynn, Emily, Danny, Kyle, and Ron, all imprisoned in another force field bubble from her ray gun, into the room. "The others were where the Sub-Leader said they would be."

"Listen to me," Andy said. "You're twisting the very meaning of the word 'peace'. Peace doesn't mean blowing up everyone that's different from you. Our worlds could learn so much from each other. Kolgan, you could be the Oort that started a shining new era of friendship and goodwill between all races in the galaxy. That could be your legacy. The greatest legacy anyone ever had. You call yourself a great leader? Well, be one now."

Lynn's eyes shined with admiration. Emily, Danny, and Kyle were also moved by their dad's passionate words.

Even Ron seemed affected. Leader Kolgan was silent. Had Andy convinced him? The rest of the Oorts watched their Leader.

Kolgan walked down the steps from his chair and stopped in front of the force field encasing Andy. He pointed at his large hat. "Of course I'm a great leader. I'm wearing the hat." The Oort leader motioned to Kezzek. "Prepare to fire." The pilot worked his control board and a powerful hum began to gain in intensity.

Andy bashed the force field with his toolbox. "Do not do this. Do not!" he shouted.

Kolgan ignored him. "Fire when ready, pilot."

Pilot Kezzek put a targeting symbol over the planet Earth. "In ten, nine, eight, seven. . ."

Andy's eyes widened in horror. The Earth—and the entire human race—was about to be turned into dust. Everyone and everything he knew was about to wiped from existence and he was powerless to do anything about it.

Or could he?

Frantically, Andy opened his toolbox and grabbed a cordless drill and a clamp. He drilled into the clamp. "Sub-Leader Nox, I'll bet you don't know what I'm doing."

"Of course I know. I know everything," said Nox with an officious smirk. "Wait, what are you doing?"

"I'm doing menial labor and you're watching! That's

what," Andy said. "I'm shaming you."

Nox spun himself around. "Make it stop! Make it stop, I tell you!" Still inside the force field, Andy was slammed into a control panel. He noticed that the panel had been dented.

The other Oorts also yelped and turned so they couldn't see. "Countdown aborted," said Kezzek, as he covered his eyes.

Andy resumed drilling into the clamp. "Even if you can't see me, you can still hear me. You all can. So degrading. How can you live with yourselves?"

Lorel dropped her ray gun and covered her ears, freeing Lynn and the others. They fell to the ground in an awkward heap.

Jarem shut his eyes and put his hands over his ears. "The Dirtlings are loose, Leader."

Kolgan jammed his hat down over his entire head. His words were muffled as he said, "I order someone to do something. I will not shame myself by doing anything."

Nox refused to drop his ray gun as he tried to cover his ears and eyes. Andy was bashed around the bridge; into the ceiling, a wall, and finally crashing hard onto Pilot Kezzek's controls.

The panel spewed colorful sparkles as Nox finally dropped his gun, releasing Andy. Harmonious alarms went off. The bridge listed and everyone floated upwards as the gravity controls went offline.

"We've lost inner gravity, engines, life support—*blor-rghattz*—all systems are fubarino," said Kezzek.

Sub-Leader Nox kept his hands over his ears. "Leader, we must abandon ship."

"Escape pod protocol," Kolgan said. "Leaders first." The agile Oorts pushed themselves off whatever wall or panel was nearest. They flew from the bridge toward the exit.

"Catch them!" Andy said.

But not even Ron's quick tentacles were fast enough to grab the frightened Oorts. On his way out, Nox inserted a key into a pad on the wall and turned it, lighting up the panel with a flashing red light. "Adios, losers."

Andy launched himself across the bridge at Kolgan. The Oort gracefully evaded him while he spoke to Lynn. "Ah, my beautiful Dancing Queen, it wasn't meant to be." The Oort Leader acrobatically passed Lynn, giving her an unwanted peck on the lips. She tried to slap him, but instead smacked Kyle across the face.

Lynn winced. "Sorry about that."

Kyle didn't hear her. He scrabbled to the bridge's exit and looked down the empty corridor. He turned to the group, panicked. "We'll never catch them. They're like little green space cheetahs."

A hissing *thwump* vibrated the bridge. Ron said, "The

escape pod has been launched."

Kyle kicked the wall he was holding on to. "Well that's great. Just great. We're screwed—we're doomed! There's no way this can get any worse."

The panel by the keyhole Nox had used changed from a steady red color to flashing red. A mellifluous tone sounded from it. *Bing, Bing, Bong. . . Bing, Bing, Bong. . . Bing, Bing, Bong. . .*

Andy looked at Ron, anchored to the wall by a few tentacles but otherwise floating with the rest of the family. "Please don't tell me that's a self-destruct countdown."

"If you say so," Ron answered. He bobbed his body in confusion. "But it does seem like information you would want to know."

twenty-one

Andy reached into his pocket where he had kept the Oort tool before remembering it was gone, destroyed, when they broke out of the Oort prison. The ship vibrated as it was pulled into the atmosphere. Ominously the Earth got closer in the view screen. "Oh, no," he said and then froze, floating in the center of the bridge.

Kyle waved an arm from where he hung onto a wall of the bridge to get Andy's attention. "Hey, this isn't the time for quiet introspection. Please do something."

"I can't," Andy said. "I can't fix it."

"Of course you can," Lynn said. "Just look at this last week."

Andy's heart hammered in his chest as the dire nature of their situation settled onto him like a mountain. "It was the Oort tool. And I broke it. I'm a fraud. I can't repair a spaceship. How could I? The engine isn't even an engine, it's more like if a pool filter and a condenser had a baby. With a sprinkler system."

"You've fixed those things a thousand times," Kyle said. "You're the only guy for this job, and more importantly, you're the only guy we've got."

"Daddy, your tools are right there," his son said, pointing. "You can fix it just like you fixed my Game Boy."

Emily pushed the floating toolbox at her father. "He's right, Dad."

Andy grabbed his tools and pushed himself to Kezzek's seat. "Ron, grab hold of everyone."

Ron gathered the floating children and handed—or tentacled—them to Lynn, who clutched them tightly. Ron then used two of his thicker tentacles to hold all three. He had a firm grip on everyone except Kyle, who scrambled away and held onto a bulkhead with both hands. "I'm good. I'm good," he said.

The alarm continued sounding in its rather soothing tones.

Bing, Bing, Bong. . . Bing, Bing, Bong. . . Bing, Bing, Bong. . .

Andy crammed himself into Kezzek's seat near the damaged panel. Nothing was lit. The pilot's controls were black and dead. "We need power, we need power," he said to himself, surveying the damage. He grabbed a mini fire extinguisher from his toolbox and sprayed a still sparking area. Andy then gestured to Ron. "Rip off this panel, please."

The alien stretched out a tentacle and tore away the blown-out panel. There were glass tubes with colored liquid inside, much like the engine, only smaller. Andy studied the area with a flashlight clamped between his teeth and felt a glimmer of hope. "It's the same. The same," he said, mumbling because of the light in his mouth.

"What's the same?" asked Lynn.

Andy took the flashlight from his mouth. "It's built like the main engine. The same pattern." One of the pipes had broken and was pumping blue liquid, which flowed down the inside of the removed panel. Andy opened his toolbox and reached for one tool before getting a better idea. He opened the weightless toolbox and all its four levels. Then he pulled the metal box itself out from underneath the individual tools. Since there was no gravity, everything floated, giving the impression that the console had flash-frozen in the middle of an explosion.

Bing, Bing, Bong. . . Bing, Bing, Bong. . . Bing, Bing, Bong. . .

Andy quickly lost himself in the work. Fasteners and removed objects lazily spun in the air where Andy placed them. His hands were deep within the console as flashlights hovered over each shoulder.

Kyle whispered as he watched. "Do a good job, do a good job. . ."

Lynn held Danny and Emily's hands tightly and Ron had them all by the waists with his tentacles. All watched as the metronomic self-destruct melody played on: *Bing, Bing, Bong. . . Bing, Bing, Bong. . . Bing, Bing, Bong. . . Bing, Bing, Bong. . . Bing, Bing, Bong. . . Bing, Bing, Bong. . .*

Kyle moved over and took one of Danny's hands. Kyle noticed he was also gripping *something* with his other hand. A quick look showed him that it was one of Ron's tentacles.

The alien looked at him pleadingly. "This is an extremely tense moment."

Kyle didn't take his hand away. "Fine."

Andy grabbed the clamps in front of him and they disappeared into the console. He plucked a small hacksaw from the air and sawed. Suddenly, a geyser of blue liquid sprayed from the panel, causing Lynn, Emily, Danny, and Kyle to yell in surprise. Another alarm added its own peppy alert to the cacophony of warning tones.

Andy didn't hear a thing. His hands moved without wasted motion or effort, snagging exactly what was needed. He stopped the squirting blue liquid and tapped the damaged pipe back into form using a wrench and ball peen hammer.

Lynn saw the Earth grow even larger in the view screen as the ship was pulled toward it. Turbulence from the atmosphere began as a low thrumming, vibrating the bridge.

"Andy. . . " she said, low and calm, although she didn't feel that way.

He didn't look back. "I know." Andy quickly plucked an acetylene torch and a sparker from his floating tools and put on goggles at the same time. He fired up the torch and grabbed a roll of soldering wire, hands again disappearing inside the panel. The torch cast his features in a harsh, staccato light.

Ron nodded to the frightened Danny and Emily. "Your father is impressive under pressure. Extremely impressive."

Andy finished soldering and wrapped the pipe in duct tape. He held his breath as the repaired pipe filled with blue liquid. "Come on, come on." Slowly, the fluid flowed in the proper direction. It glowed, taking on a bright neon blue color. The rest of the liquids inside the panel recovered their vibrant hues. It was working. One by one the orange warning lights winked off.

The alarms ceased whining. . . except one.

Bing, Bing, Bong. . . Bing, Bing, Bong. . . Bing, Bing, Bong. . .

The lights on the panels in front of Kezzek's chair switched on. Gravity returned to the bridge. With a clatter, Andy's tools fell from the air. Ron's tenacious grip on the ceiling prevented everyone he held from taking a spill. He lowered himself and the others onto the floor.

"You da man!" Kyle said. "Best handyman ever." Flames licked at the view screen and the ship shook with more urgency. "But now we're on fire. Why are we on fire?"

"The atmosphere is getting thicker," said Ron. "We will burn up if we do not slow ourselves."

Kyle's shoulders slumped. "Of course we will."

The single alarm didn't stop. *Bing, Bing, Bong. . . Bing, Bing, Bong. . . Bing, Bing, Bong. . .*

"Okay, the engines are working," said Andy "All I have to do is—" Bull moose realization hit him. He had to *fly* the ship. "I don't know how to fly the ship," he said to himself.

"Danny does," said Emily.

Lynn shushed her. "Quiet, Emily, your father is thinking."

Andy also dismissed his daughter for a second, but then— "Wait, what did you say?" Andy looked over at Emily, who pointed at Danny. He was terrified and hugged Lynn tightly as the vibrations grew exponentially.

"If the engine was the same, maybe the controls on

the game are, too," Emily said. "And he's been playing the game a lot."

"Danny, do you know how to fly the ship?" asked Andy.

The view screen was covered with flames and the ship was shaking itself apart.

"I don't know," his son said, crying a little. "Maybe."

"You can do it, Danny," said his sister. "Don't be scared. I'll even let you on my side of the room when we get back home."

"Whenever I want?" he asked.

"Whenever you want."

Danny let go of Lynn. Ron lifted him to Andy, who kissed him on the forehead and wiped away his tears. "Let's play. Show me how to do it."

Danny took out his Gameboy and compared it to Pilot Kezzek's control board. He sniffled and pointed at the controls one by one as the bridge bucked and heaved. They were duplicated on his handheld video game's screen. "That one moves it up and down, that one, left and right. There's the gas, and that one's the brakes."

Kyle held onto Leader Kolgan's chair as best he could. "I think we should use the brakes."

Andy did that and the ship slowed. The flames along the view screen lessened, then disappeared, replaced by the solid white of clouds. The shaking subsided and the ship flew as smoothly as if they were flying. Which they were.

Clouds obscured the view screen but everyone relaxed for a moment.

"Not so bad now, huh?" Andy said.

The spaceship broke through the clouds and—

Hurtled toward a building! Everyone yelled their lungs out as Andy put the craft into a shrieking turn. Ron clutched his family as they were whipped sideways.

"Whoa, that was Denver. Which means, yeah, there's the 93," Andy said, trying to keep calm.

The alarm klaxon grew louder and more insistent.

BING-BING-BONG, BING-BING-BONG, BING-BING-BONG, BING-BING-BONG...

"I hate to be the sayer of bad tidings," Ron said. "But we need to land. The self-destruct will happen soon."

The trees came closer and closer in the view screen as Andy babied the controls, making adjustments. "Okay, easy. . . easy. . . " The spaceship screamed over the road. The laser cannon had melted to a nub from the heat of their reentry. Andy tried to put the craft on the road but it was going way too fast. It hit the highway and skipped over a billboard, back into the air, and whipped toward the woods when the road veered off in another direction.

Deputy Bob was sound asleep behind the billboard, ostensibly waiting to catch speeders. He was startled awake by the mad beeping of his detector. The radar told him "579 MPH." There was nothing in sight so Bob grumbled and turned it off, settling in for more shut-eye. He had had a tough night.

Andy managed to slow the ship and crash-land in a somewhat controlled manner, though there was a jagged tear in the hull. The scales on the outer hull zigzagged frenetically as various ruptures hissed and coughed. The self-destruct klaxon became deafening.

. . . *BING-BING-BONG, BING-BING-BONG, BING-BING-BONG.* . .

The hole in the side of the ship made it much easier for everyone to get out. Kyle stumbled out on wobbly legs and kissed the ground. "Thank you."

Andy gave Emily and Danny to Lynn and helped Kyle to his feet. "Get behind those rocks," he told everyone.

. . . *BING-BING-BONG, BING-BING-BONG, BING-BING-BONG.* . .

Lynn, Emily, and Danny ducked behind the formation. Andy heaved Kyle over before diving after him.

. . . *BING-BING-BONG, BING-BING-BONG, BING-BING-BONG.* . .

In no hurry, Ron made his way outside.

"Ron, run!" Andy yelled. "The self-destruct! The self-destruct!"

BONG!BONG!BONG!BONG!BONG!BONG!-
BONG!BONG!BONG!BONG!BONG!

Ron seemed fine with this, happy, in fact. He turned to watch, standing not ten feet away from the Oort ship. "Yes, it's about to." The alarm stopped and the spaceship evaporated. The metal dissolved skyward in a beautiful display of multi-colored sparkles, disappearing with a fizzing noise. Ron glided over to Andy and his exhausted group. "Are self-destruct and destruct not different words in your language?"

Andy laughed as he hugged Lynn and the kids.

"Dad, I don't wanna go to space camp," said Emily.

"That's okay by me," Andy said and they hugged some more.

twenty-two

One year later, Andy and Lynn did the dishes—by hand—in front of their brand new dishwasher. Yes, it was used occasionally when they were strapped for time but Andy found he enjoyed their cleaning routine too much to give it up. And he liked their time together, as his own workload had vastly increased. On this particular day the washing and drying process was inefficiently, and wonderfully, delayed by joking around and a tickle fight. They had to stop when the racket in the other room made by Emily and Danny became too loud to ignore.

"Kids!" Andy said.

Emily and Danny came into the kitchen. "We're not

fighting, Dad. Our characters are."

Danny nodded, backing his sister up. "Yeah, I'm helping her memorize lines for a fight scene in the school play. It's fun."

Andy looked at his wife to make sure this was okay and she nodded. "Carry on, then."

The kids left. After he put the last dish in the cupboard, Andy gave Lynn a kiss on the cheek and headed toward the door. "Don't forget about Spree," Lynn said.

"I would not miss it, my sweet, sweet Dancing Queen," he said.

Andy drove Justine to the warehouse area at the edge of town; the same place where he had drag raced Kyle what seemed like a lifetime ago. It had turned out to be the perfect place for his new repair shop.

He parked in front of a warehouse with a giant Handy Andy sign. Andy took out his key and unlocked the door. The door was always locked, even during business hours. There wasn't a soul around, but you could never be too careful.

Inside the warehouse was a large auto bay with multiple hydraulic lifts on which lay alien spacecraft. Andy grabbed a translator from a rack and hung it around his neck as he walked in. They had gotten the translators in six months ago (with Ron's considerable help), and they had really helped business.

Kyle argued with a rail-thin gray alien whose name

was Gorp. He was an Idoktal and had been to the shop a few times. His outfit—overalls and soiled hat—matched the ensemble of truckers (literally) everywhere. Gorp gestured at his ugly mid-range hauler. The translators enabled everyone to understand each other quite well and allowed Andy to hear the conversation perfectly. "I come in for a dilithium boost and now I need a new proton chamber?" wheezed Gorp. That was what his species did on Earth when speaking, as they usually breathed methane. "What kind of clip shop is this?"

"Gorp, don't put this on me. You're the one flying your rig through wormholes," said Kyle. Andy chuckled as he passed.

Ron dealt with two Jahvvian customers Andy hadn't seen before. They were squat with bluish skin, and youngsters for their kind. Their ship was an elegant sports craft model and had a dented fender.

"It's a Gulternal Vorkin," said one of the two. "Only four hundred were ever made. Our Dad's gonna kill us."

"We heard you guys are the best in the sector," the other said. "Please. Help us."

Ron had five tentacles working on the ship; another held a clipboard, and a third, coffee. Like Kyle, he wore a pair of Handy Andy overalls with his name sewn on the pocket. It went entirely across his chest, but the *Ron* of it was highlighted, as other beings besides Andy and

Kyle also had problems with the pronunciation of his full name.

"Do not worry, younglings," Ron said. "It shall look like new."

Andy went to a rack of different toolboxes. He opened one to check that all the proper tools were inside. Many of his newer ones were alien in nature, another perk of having Ron as a partner. He had no less than *three* Oortian baton tools.

Ron motioned with yet another tentacle to Andy. "They're waiting. Rush job."

He took the toolbox off the rack. "What else is new?"

Andy walked to one of the two gravity lifts and got on. Pressing a remote, the disk took him up to the ceiling where a Kyldenn shunt dilated a hole in the ceiling so he could stand on the roof. Andy checked that all his sight and signal jammers were working properly. They were, so he sent an all clear signal burst. His customers counted on him for stress free repairs, after all.

In a moment, his translator crackled. "This is Scah-tay of the Collective. Sorry about the short notice, Andy. We have no idea what's wrong. It's a mess, I tell you."

A stadium-sized spaceship became visible overhead. The craft was beyond impressive. But today, this marvel of alien engineering had an engine that sputtered and crackled instead of humming the way it should.

"Sure thing," Andy said. He grinned. "Beam me up, Scah-tay."

A gravity lift moved him upwards to the twinkling underside entry port of the ship. He looked down at the roof of his building. The running lights on the alien ship reflected off his special *other* sign. This one was visible from the stars and could be read several parsecs away. It read "Handy Andy—Lowest Prices in the Galaxy," and listed his services in thousands of alien languages. It brought him a lot of work. Maybe even a little too much. But Andy Robinson was a handyman, just like his father before him, and he could not have been happier.

epilogue

The tiny, dented Oort escape pod tumbled end over end. Inside, Leader Kolgan, Sub-Leader Nox, Senior Science Officer Jarem, Junior Science Officer Lorel, and Pilot Kezzek stared at each other, each strapped into their chairs. The pod was divided with masking tape into five equal areas. No one did anything about the steady beeping noise coming from one of the panels.

With their hair longer and uniforms dingy, the Oorts did not look their best. "Mangy" was a word that had been bandied about. Nox and Kezzek sported bruises on their faces from their numerous fights. Finally, with a disinterested stab of his finger, Nox pressed a button and the beeping stopped. Everyone looked at Kolgan.

"What is the condition of the pod?" asked the Oort leader.

"Identical to yesterday and the day before, et cetera, et cetera," Nox said. "We have no power and continue to drift."

"I order someone to fix it," Kolgan said.

The Sub-Leader looked around the escape pod. "Is anyone willing to do menial labor? I, myself, am a definite *no*." Jarem purred in frustration. Nox glared at him. "Is that you volunteering, Science Boy?"

"Of course not," huffed Jarem. "The nerve of you."

Nox checked with Lorel and she shook her head.

"Nope," said Kezzek. "But I'd kill for a waffle cone. Literally, Nox. I'd kill you for a waffle cone."

Nox and Kezzek purr-growled, unbuckled their seatbelts, and went at each other. They fought their way around the small cabin, weightless and ping-ponging from side to side.

Jarem sighed and his antennae drooped. "And here we go again. Why don't you do some actual *leading*, Leader?"

Kolgan growled. "Jarem, shut your juice drain. I order everyone back to their areas. I said stop. I command it!"

Lorel tugged at her collar as Nox and Kezzek bounced off the wall next to the one tiny viewport in the escape pod. "Is it getting warmer in here?"

Nox and Kezzek stopped fighting. Everyone jostled for a position around the viewport.

Outside they saw a blazing sun. "Uh-oh."

THE END

ACKNOWLEDGMENTS

Thanks to my editor Barbara Randall Kesel for her numerous fine ideas and most importantly pulling me back when I went off the rails. (*Randy* Andy Saves the World is a completely different book.) Interior and cover layout are by the very talented Torborg Davern. I love my little spaceship dingbats. And I am ever so grateful to artist Hillary Bauman for creating a great cover with the barest guidance ("Maybe a guy and a spaceship?") mixed with more than a little gibberish (Make it actiony, but awesome. You know, like, 'Arrgh! Look out!'")

. . . I am so embarrassed.

Here comes the shameless plug section. Feel free to skip this.

If you liked the book I'd really appreciate a review. It doesn't have to be on Amazon or the internet, maybe just tell a friend (but Amazon would be fantastic).

Questions? Comments? Bring 'em on. You can reach me on Facebook at EJ Altbacker, on twitter @ejaltbacker, and (fingers crossed) on my author site EJAltbacker.com sometime in 2015. Dates and locations of my appearances, info about my next projects, and news about the cartoons and shows I'm writing can be found there.

Thanks and Happy Reading!

—EJ Altbacker

EJ Altbacker is a screenwriter whose credits include such television shows as Spooksville, Green Lantern: The Animated Series, Spider-Man, Ben 10, Jay Jay the Jet Plane, Mucha Lucha, and Static Shock. He holds an MFA in screenwriting from the American Film Institute and an undergraduate degree from the University of Notre Dame. EJ lives in Hermosa Beach, California, and enjoys biking and plodding (his word for jogging as he's pretty slow) by the beach.

Cover artist Hillary Bauman is a California native and Chapman University graduate. She creates art for stage, film, and graphic novels. You can see more of her work at www.thechromabear.com

53993715R00099

Made in the USA
Charleston, SC
21 March 2016